TAMA

by

PRIYA HEIN

Tamarin Bay, Mauritius, is a travel agent's paradise: a tropical ocean, fishermen unloading their daily catch, children building sandcastles, surfers riding giant waves. But just along the shoreline is the beach of La Preneuse, the taker of souls. The island is haunted with tragedy and the remnants of colonial rule.

But it is also home, where Anita Ram longs to be following the collapse of her marriage. After enduring a shocking betrayal and the sexism and racism of a cold Britain in the early twenty-first century, she finds comfort in simple things: her mother's cooking, her childhood bedroom and a handsome architect.

Will these be enough for Anita to find happiness again, or will the ghosts of her past consume her?

Following the international success of her debut *Riambel*, Hein's heart-wrenching new novel reveals the violence and beauty inherent in her native Mauritius.

© Cale Stelken

ABOUT THE AUTHOR

PRIYA HEIN is a Mauritian author whose first novel, *Riambel*, won the Prix Athéna 2023 and the Jean Fanchette Prize 2021.

She was nominated for the 2017 Astrid Lindgren Memorial Award, shortlisted for the Prix de l'Atelier Littéraire in 2021 and the Miles Morland Scholarship in 2023, and participated in the 2024 Iowa International Writing Program (IWP) fall residency. Priya lives in Mauritius with her family.

TAMARIN

PRIYA HEIN

THE
INDIGO
PRESS

THE INDIGO PRESS
50 Albemarle Street
London W1S 4BD
www.theindigopress.com

The Indigo Press Publishing Limited Reg. No. 10995574
Registered Office: Wellesley House, Duke of Wellington Avenue,
Royal Arsenal, London SE18 6SS

First published in Great Britain in 2025 by the Indigo Press

A CIP catalogue record for this book is available from the British Library.

This is a work of fiction. Names, characters, places and incidents are
products of the author's imagination or are used fictionally and are
not to be construed as real. Any resemblance to actual events, locales,
organisations, or persons, living or dead, is entirely coincidental.

ISBN: 978-1-911648-93-2
eBook ISBN: 978-1-911648-94-9

Excerpt from 'Devant la Mer' on p.141 by Robert Edward Hart from the collection
Mer Indienne (1925) reproduced with the kind permission of Stefan Hart de Keating

Cover design © Luke Bird
Cover artwork © Mila Gupta
Art direction by House of Thought
Typeset by Tetragon, London
Printed and bound by CPI (UK) Ltd, Croydon CR0 4YY

MIX
Paper | Supporting
responsible forestry
FSC
www.fsc.org
FSC® C013604

EU GPSR authorised representative
Logos Europe, 9 rue Nicolas Poussin, 17000, La Rochelle, France
e-mail: contact@logoseurope.eu

1 3 5 7 9 8 6 4 2

For my mother, Indira, who taught me
how to swim so that I wouldn't sink.

All sorrows can be borne if you put them into a story.

KAREN BLIXEN

Douce plage où naquit mon âme
Et toi, savane en fleurs
Que l'Océan trempe de pleurs
Et le soleil de flamme.

Sweet beach where my soul was born
And you, blooming savannah
Soaked by the tears of the ocean
And the blazing sun.

PAUL-JEAN TOULET
(translated by Priya Hein)

PROLOGUE

Time has slowed down. The hours stretch ahead like an infinite ocean, its waves threatening to wash over her until she's drowning. She eventually leaves the empty house and heads towards the nearest travel agency, ankles deep in decaying leaves, oblivious to the world around her.

A few minutes later, she reaches the high street and realizes that the office is closed. She desperately bangs on the door, hoping someone will still be in.

'A ticket to Mauritius. Leaving as soon as possible!'

But her plea remains unheard. Nose pressed against the cold windowpane, she notices a beach holiday advert among a display of Alpine ski resorts. She immediately recognizes the mountain range tucked behind the bay of Tamarin, also known as the mythical bay. She longs to see that familiar stretch of blue again. Her memories of that little piece of paradise are dreamlike, simultaneously vivid and vaporous.

'I just want to go home,' she says to no one in particular. With a heavy heart she pulls away from the window.

On her way back, she passes an off-licence with a flashing neon sign and decides to buy a little pick-me-up to get her through the bitter night.

'A bottle of Red Label, please,' she says to the shopkeeper, whose glassy eyes are glued to a portable television. The man barely looks at her as she hands over a crumpled twenty-pound note.

Cradling the bottle inside her coat like a newborn, she ignores a bunch of youngsters smoking and drinking lager straight from the can. For the rest of the walk she keeps her eyes downcast, lost in her own world.

Once back at the house, she lights a vanilla-scented candle and runs herself a bubble bath. While waiting for the bath to fill, she opens the newly bought bottle and pours herself a generous serving. The liquid burns her throat, but she keeps on drinking. After polishing off her drink, she takes the rest of the bottle to the bathroom. Once the bath is filled to the brim, she drops her clothes on the sleek marble floor and glides into the frothy water.

When she closes her eyes, she breathes in the humidity and hears the wind rustling through the tamarind leaves overlooking the bay. The sun softly caressing her face. Soon she will be home. Back on her island, her motherland, where the gentle breeze from the sea saw her enter this world.

I

It would have been quicker to hail a taxi from the airport, but Anita wasn't yet ready to face her mother. Or anyone else, for that matter. She took the bus instead, an old rattling vehicle similar to those she had been used to as a child. Upon landing, it had been oddly comforting to listen to the casual banter of airport workers who had just finished their early-morning shift. It had been a while since she had heard anyone speak in Creole, her mother tongue, the dialect of former slaves and Indian servants. The language of the oppressed. Spoken but unwritten. Unrecorded.

As she stepped out of the crowded bus, she was hit by the sickly-sweet smell of molasses being processed into raw sugar. It was harvest season. The air felt heavy and slightly smoky from the fumes of the nearby factory. The sky was peppered with cotton-wool clouds through which the midday sun was shining. The change of scenery was in stark contrast to the world she had left behind.

Acres and acres of sugar cane fields rolled towards the ocean below. The lush plantation belonged to an estate that had employed several generations of her family, including her Indian ancestors who after the abolition of slavery had crossed the Kala Pani, the black waters, as indentured labourers.

From the bus stop, she walked down the road, slowly taking everything in while dragging her small, battered suitcase behind. Past the village school, named after her great-uncle who used to teach there, and past the corner shop, before finally turning right into the residential lane. A few seconds later, as she approached the rusty gate, she caught a glimpse of the old cement house. It looked even more dilapidated than she remembered. When she was a child, the house had seemed grander, more imposing. It had stood out from the neighbouring houses. Now it looked lost among the vulgar, charmless constructions which were being hastily erected to house extended families.

The wrought-iron gate creaked feebly as she let herself in. The basil plants and marigolds, used for prayers, still lined the pathway leading to the house. A faint tune was floating out of a nearby radio. It was a song from an old Bollywood movie Ma was fond of. Everything felt familiar and yet strange at the same time. She caught a whiff of curry as she tiptoed inside the house, lugging her suitcase into the narrow corridor leading to the kitchen.

Even though the kitchen door was open, she hesitated before gently knocking on its wooden frame to announce her arrival. Ma looked up in surprise, as if she had seen a ghost. She was sitting on a plastic chair that was too small for her, busy slicing vegetables. Something was quietly brewing in the casserole on the stove. 'Anita!' she exclaimed, with a sharp intake of breath. A sudden softness slipped into the older woman's eyes.

They stared at one another for a few seconds. Once Anita saw Ma's kind and concerned face, she could no longer contain the emotions she had been withholding. She finally broke down. The agony of the last few weeks all came flooding back. Tears streamed down her cheeks as she wept.

'Hush, beti.' Ma sprang up from her chair to embrace Anita. She held on tightly as if Anita would otherwise float away, gently stroking her daughter's lustreless hair.

'It's all right now. You're home.'

Feeling Ma's protective arms around her frail body unleashed another burst of emotion. Anita sobbed uncontrollably, head down, shoulders pressed towards her mother's. It had been a while since she had been touched with anything approaching tenderness. It was hard to know how long they stayed like this. She lost all sense of time and space. All she knew was that she was back home. Unburdened.

'Why didn't you call? We would have picked you up from the airport,' Ma gently reproached. She wiped her daughter's face with the loose, frayed end of her cotton sari.

Anita began to feel more composed as the tears subsided. 'I only decided yesterday morning. I barely had time to pack.'

Ma eyed the suitcase abandoned in a corner of the room. 'Is that all?' she asked.

'I only packed my books.'

'What about clothes?'

'I have enough to wear for a couple of days. If not, I'll pick up a few things at the bazaar. I don't need much.'

'You've lost weight,' observed Ma.

'I've not been hungry lately.'

'Never mind. We'll fix that. It's good to see you, beti. It's been too long,' said Ma. She handed her a cup of sweet vanilla tea. Anita gratefully accepted it and, while sipping, watched Ma mix chickpea flour for vegetable fritters.

'How long are you staying?' Ma ventured delicately.

Anita shrugged. 'Don't know. For a while, I guess.'

'What about work?'

'I took unpaid leave.' Anita tried not to think about her career as she idly fingered the scalloped edge of the plastic tablecloth.

'I can't believe that appalling English husband of yours would do such a thing!' Ma spat as she threw the vegetables into a pot of boiling oil that sizzled and sputtered. The room instantly filled with a smoky haze. 'How could he? Your own flesh and blood!' The older woman opened the window, trying to wave out the fog.

'Ma, please. I don't want to talk about Paul. I've had a very long flight. I'm tired. I think I'll go to bed.'

The grease hissed into silence.

'Yes. You need to rest, but eat some of this first.' Ma handed Anita a plate of piping-hot vegetable fritters, charred at the edges, and added a dollop of chutney on the side. 'Let me get you a towel and clear away some things in your old room.' She got up, leaving Anita on her own to toy with her food and listen to the melancholic Indian music. Although she could not grasp the full meaning of the lyrics, she recognized it as a ghazal about forbidden love.

Her mother came back a few minutes later with a fresh towel and a bar of soap still in its wrapper. Her eyes rested briefly on the plate of soggy untouched fritters and the lump of brown chutney that was starting to look gooey.

Anita pushed the plate away. 'I'm not hungry.'

'You should eat something.'

Anita shook her head in response. Food was the last thing on her mind.

With a sigh, Ma took the plate and scraped the untouched food into a plastic container, for later.

'Please don't tell anyone I'm back. I can't deal with seeing anyone at the moment. At least for a couple of days.'

'What about your sister?' Ma looked up from her task.

'Especially Didi.' Anita lowered her gaze and studied her bare feet.

'You really should talk to her, but fine. I won't tell a soul until you're ready. Just remember that it's a small island. People will find out soon enough. *Zot kontan palab.* The villagers' tongues know no bounds.'

As Anita got up, an endless fatigue swept her whole being. Overcome with an urgent desire to sleep and forget, she barely managed to brush her teeth before climbing into her childhood bed. She switched off the bedside lamp, filling the small room with darkness.

2

Ma gently nudged her.

Anita woke up from her slumber, slightly disoriented as she scanned the unfamiliar surroundings. The house that was once home was now somehow foreign.

Her throat felt dry. 'How long did I sleep?'

'It's almost midday.' Ma placed a glass of water and a cup of tea on the bedside table. The older woman pulled open the curtains, flooding the room with light. Anita squinted.

As soon as Anita's mother left, she threw back the sheets and went to the window. In one swift, brusque movement, she drew them back to block out the offending light, before crawling back into her saggy bed. Despite the tropical heat, she buried herself in the warmth of the crumpled sheets, retreating further and further under the blanket. It was tempting to drown herself in its creases and folds and never have to face the cruel glare of daylight again.

A couple of hours later, Anita heard the hem of Ma's sari swishing on the floor as she tiptoed barefoot towards the bed. She carefully placed a plastic tray on the bedside table and replaced the glass of water with a fresh one.

'Beti. You should eat something. I've made you some dal.'

Anita lay motionless on her bed, pretending to be asleep.

'I usually go to the bazaar on Saturdays. Do you need anything?'

'No thanks,' Anita eventually replied in a faint muffle from beneath the bedspread.

'I'll be back within a couple of hours.' Ma closed the door behind her, leaving her daughter to endure the silence of the house. To breathe in the emptiness, the pathetic heaving of her own breath punctuated by long sighs that came from somewhere deep inside.

Anita could not remember the last time she had slept. Really slept, without suffering from the same vivid nightmares.

She must have dozed off again, for she was woken by Ma's discreet steps on the vinyl floor as she came back from the bazaar. Anita could picture Ma removing her flip-flops before entering the house, lugging her panie full of fresh vegetables. She heard her shuffling about in the kitchen, unpacking groceries. A little later, Ma tiptoed into the bedroom with another cup of tea and placed it on the bedside table before leaving as quietly as she had come in.

Anita sat up in bed. She contemplated the two cups positioned next to each other. An unattractive skin had formed on the hardly touched tea, floating aimlessly on the surface of the murky liquid the dead colour of gangrene. An inviting smell of vanilla rose from the freshly brewed tea, which Ma had served in a pale, chipped mug.

Picking up the cup, she crossed the room and pulled the curtains wide open. With one swift movement, she tossed the cold tea out of the window, creating a long, dark stain on the reddish earth. The shape of the liquid, stark against the dry soil, reminded her of a snake.

As Anita sipped the sweet, milky tea, she gazed out of the window in search of the earlier imprint on the ground. The liquid already seemed to have evaporated in the heat of the scorching sun, leaving behind only a faint mark.

3

The next day, Anita felt strangely liberated to wake up in her childhood bed instead of in the oversized one she and Paul used to share in Stoke Newington. The ten thousand kilometres that separated her from London offered a sense of detachment, physically and emotionally, for which she was grateful.

A feeble light played on the wall, cast by the December sun streaming in through the window. She could hear the shrieks of children from the nearby kindergarten and Ma pottering about in the kitchen making khir. Woven through it all was the hum of insects and greetings of chirping bulbuls. The familiar smells and sounds of home.

Anita stared at the ceiling, recognizing the same cracks on the wall and the light fixture hanging from the aged plaster. Paint was beginning to peel off in layers. The faded yellowish walls bore greasy Blu-Tack marks where her posters, torn from magazines, had once hung. Her fingers gently stroked the patchwork bedcover which her grandma had sown using leftover scrap material, pieces cut out of Anita's old dresses and Ma's silk saris. It carried a faint whiff of incense sticks from her mother's daily prayers and offerings to numerous effigies of Hindu goddesses.

The shelves were heavily loaded with dusty schoolbooks and notepads plagued with the omnipresent mildew. When Anita was fifteen, the pink frilly curtains had seemed the height of elegance. Now they looked sad, their tulle grown dark with dust, their colour bleached out by the sun.

Her former school uniform, an old-fashioned checked blue pinafore and a stiff white blouse, still hung miserably in the creaky wardrobe whose missing door no one had cared to repair. In some ways, it was as if she had never left Mauritius. Perhaps she could erase the past. Pretend it never happened.

The next couple of days were dull and sedated. Anita moped around the house, drifting from room to room. From her window, she stared silently at the clouds for hours on end. Occasionally, she would take a battered book from the shelf and absent-mindedly leaf through the pages tunnelled by worms before putting it back with a sigh.

Anita eventually succumbed to Ma's entreaties ('A change of scenery will do you good') and ventured out of the house into the daylight.

The bus was not crowded at that time of the day. She fished in her bag for some loose change. Having handed over a few rupees to the bus conductor, she found a prickly seat at the back, next to a grimy window. There was a girl sitting nearby, eyes closed, impervious to the world outside, moving her head to something only she could hear. The rattling ride took almost an hour, but Anita did not care. Her musty, dog-eared copy of *Le bal du dodo* lay on her lap, untouched as she watched the world go by.

At Rivière Noire, she stepped out of the vehicle in front of a Chinese shop with a red corrugated-iron roof and headed towards Allée des Pêcheurs. The tiny colonial post office next to the century-old banyan tree was just as she remembered. Next to it was the cemetery where she used to play hide-and-seek with her cousins, where they'd dared each other to hide behind the tombs of famous corsairs and the tamarind trees buried at the back. Her older sister had never joined in their childish games, because she didn't wish to be seen with Anita. The ten-year gap between them had carved a natural rift between the siblings. It was only years later, when Anita was almost an adult, that she discovered that Ma had miscarried twins after the birth of her older sister. She often wondered how it would have been to grow up with two more siblings, instead of only an all-knowing, distant sister who constantly looked down on her.

She walked past a bed-and-breakfast sign with a blue butterfly before arriving at the secluded La Preneuse beach facing the ancient Martello Tower. Breathing in the dry, salty air, she could hear the sea long before it unfurled itself before her. A sudden gust of wind carried a flurry of sand and ocean spray into her eyes, dusting her with salt. As she watched the waves break at her feet, a conch shell washed up on the shore. Remembering an old sea legend, she placed the hollow part next to her right ear: the murmurings of the ocean were like distant echoes of a long-lost dream.

There were not many tourists on the beach despite it being peak season – just a handful of employees enjoying their mid-morning break and some retired fishermen slapping down dominoes and drinking cans of Phoenix beer under the shade of a casuarina.

Anita sat on an empty bench and stared out at the sea, engulfed in her thoughts. For a long time, she observed the boats beyond the reef, specks of white dotting the scintillating blue lagoon. Every now and then she brushed away the tears that found their way down her cheeks. Eventually, she opened her straw bag and fished out the plastic container Ma had packed before she had left the house. It was filled with vegetable samosas and chilli fritters. After nibbling on one or two, she threw the crumbs to nearby birds.

She carried on staring at the mesmerizing blue until she felt compelled to get up. Without thinking, she kicked off her sandals, peeled off her T-shirt and jeans and waded into the cool, inviting water. After a few lengths of breaststroke, she allowed herself to float on her back, arms spread wide open, face turned towards the sky. Submerged as she was by the ocean's bewitching gravity, the world around her was still except for the quiet hum of the sea. Exerting as little energy as possible, Anita dived underneath its skin. Floating in the familiar sea-blue silence, her limbs were buoyant and loose. Like the dead.

Her body emerged from the water feeling somewhat lighter, as if the sea had washed away some of her sorrows. After the bland grey skies of London, it was pleasing to bathe in the clear water, to dry herself off in the warm sand, offering her face to the sun, soaking it in while tasting the salt on her lips.

A few minutes later, someone softly nudged her. Anita opened her eyes to find a little girl staring at her with curiosity. She looked like an angel in her pristine white dress, a stark contrast to her copper-toned, cherubic face. A mass of golden hair floated like a halo around her head.

'Look what I caught!' The seraphic child was proudly holding up a bucket. There was something pure about her that touched Anita.

The girl was staring at her expectantly, so Anita politely peered into the small plastic bucket. 'A starfish! It's beautiful!' she cooed at the perfectly shaped sea creature at the bottom of the pail.

In response, the girl beamed with pride.

'What's your name?'

'My name's Maya.' She spoke with a slight twang, which Anita was unable to place straight away.

'I'm Anita. Nice to meet you, Maya. Where did you find this beauty?'

'There, by the rocks.' The child turned right and pointed her spade towards the bay.

'Maya is a such a lovely name.'

The girl looked pleased.

'Do you know what it means?'

Maya shook her head.

'It means "illusion" in Sanskrit.'

The child looked at her blankly.

'An illusion is like a dream,' Anita said.

When she looked up, a male figure was heading in their direction. She assumed it was the girl's father. There was a surreal look about him. His white linen shirt flapping in the breeze reminded her of a sailing boat gliding on water.

Anita suddenly felt self-conscious wearing nothing but her black underwear. Her earlier lack of inhibition melted away and was replaced by the traditional prudishness she had been brought up with. She quickly got up and shook off the specks of sand before pulling on her jeans and T-shirt. 'It's getting late. I must go. It was nice to meet you, Maya. Goodbye.' She grabbed her sandals and bag from the sand.

'Auf Wiedersehen!' shouted the girl as she proudly ran towards the man to show off her prized catch.

The next day, Anita caught a bus to the same beach, where she could hide from her mother and her probing questions. The secluded bay provided her with an anonymity her home village could not offer. It was her sanctuary, at least during the day. She felt comfortable among the tourists, expats and seasoned fishermen with weather-beaten faces going about their daily business.

Nobody knew her there. It was a place where she could wallow in her misery, away from judgements and questions about her failed marriage. Where she could plunge into bouts of introspection. She could let the tears mingle with seawater, every single drop a recrimination, reminding her of what she had lost: her husband, her job, her self-respect, her ability to see the future, her sanity. Her life. The last thing she wanted was for anyone to see her desolation.

A fisherman was busy unloading his pirogue on the shore, not far from the bay. The man, who had a distorted tattoo of a dolphin on his upper arm, was squatting on the sand, using the flat part of a rock as a makeshift table. An old handkerchief was tied in knots around his head like a bandana. With one hand, he pulled a parrotfish out of a recycled canister filled with seawater. The creature flapped its tail as the fisherman tried to flatten it out on the stone, and kept on struggling for its life right until the sharp edge of the knife tore into its belly. The deep cut exposed guts that spilled out. Using both hands, the fisherman ripped the slit wide open and scooped out its insides. He pulled out the heart and threw it back into the water before hacking off the head in one brutal movement.

Anita watched the fish, now dismembered, as it lay motionless – spots of translucent rainbow against granite, murky seawater stained with blood. The combination of the heat and the smell of seaweed and dead fish was making her feel nauseous. She had to escape.

4

Groggy following a restless night, Anita eased herself out of bed and reached for the pile of crumpled clothes on the floor. She slipped out of the house again. The humidity pressed against her shoulders as she wandered the empty streets, unsure of what she was looking for or where she was going. Attracted by a thin plume of smoke coming from the end of the village, she trudged through the sugar cane fields, trying to find shade under the mango trees along the way.

After following a dirt track, she found herself in front of a gate leading to a temple at the foot of the Corps de Garde. The colour of the temple walls, probably once a bright shade of fuchsia, had faded after years of rain, sun and neglect. The floor was littered with debris: incense sticks, a discarded plastic bag, bits of discoloured bunting and a scattering of dead leaves. Something scurried away across the floor. A rat? A field mouse? Or perhaps a tang from the nearby plantation? It was hard to tell in the shade.

Anita opened the creaky metal gate and walked up the narrow stairs with missing railings until she was greeted by a life-size statue of a blue-faced Krishna playing his flute. His neck was wreathed with a garland of fresh marigolds. The air was heavily scented with camphor and burned sandalwood. Enshrined on the altar were Hanuman, the monkey god, and Ganesh, the half-elephant, half-human god.

'Can I help you, beti?'

A skeletal-looking pandit appeared from the back room holding a set of wooden prayer beads. He wore nothing but a loosely wrapped saffron-coloured loincloth. His greasy face was pockmarked. It was strange to be referred to as beti, daughter, by a man who looked only a couple of years older than her.

'I was just passing by,' she said, caught off guard.

'Shall I perform a service for you?'

Anita shrugged.

'*Thik hai, beti.*'

The pandit placed his prayer beads on a table next to the altar and started to assemble a few items for the puja. He rang a little copper handbell and sprinkled some holy water on Anita before reciting a mantra with his eyes shut in concentration. After a final orison for her well-being, he dipped his finger into a small terracotta pot and painted a dot of bright vermilion between her eyes.

'May you find peace, my child.'

The pandit looked at Anita expectantly as she pushed away a single strand of hair that had got stuck in the red paste on her forehead, smudging the tikka on her face. She dug into her pocket and found some coins, which she dropped into the donation box prominently displayed in front of the altar.

'Dhanyavad.' Satisfied with the clink of coins hitting metal, the skinny man thanked her and uttered a few more verses in Sanskrit before picking up his prayer beads again, leaving Anita free to go back downstairs and roam about in the empty courtyard.

Preparations for some kind of function were under way behind the temple. A couple of men were clearing the site, poking hot embers and scooping old ashes into a pail. It was only when she saw the freshly stacked wood a few metres away that she made the connection with the Hindu ritual of antyesti, the last sacrifice.

Distracted by the distant sound of chanting, Anita looked up to find a retinue of male mourners carrying a palanquin covered in fresh palm leaves and flowers. The procession of chanting men was slowly making its way through the fields towards the back of the temple. The chief mourner was whispering a mantra into the dead person's ears:

> *Ram naam satya hai*
> *Ram naam satya hai*
> *Ram naam satya hai*
> *Ram naam satya hai*
> *Ram naam satya hai*

This mantra rippled through the crowd. It was eerie for Anita to hear her family name being chanted over and over to absolve the dead of their bad deeds in life.

The corpse bearers' faces dripped with sweat as they struggled with the morning heat and the weight of the pallet on their shoulders. A palm frond fell on the ground, exposing the naked skeleton of bamboo. From behind a tree, Anita watched the palanquin being placed on the stack of dry logs, the dead person's feet facing south in accordance with traditional rites.

A reverent hush fell over the crowd as the lead mourner walked around the pyre. He recited mantras and sprinkled the corpse and the wood with ghee before setting them alight. As he took a step back, the wooden stack went up. The roaring flames danced wildly to the chanting of the mourners as their voices reached a crescendo.

> *Om shanti shanti shanti. Om shanti. Om.*

Anita wondered if the dead ever really left, and if so, where they went.

From her hiding place, Anita stood mesmerized by the scene unfolding before her, until a sharp voice behind her made her jump. A man, who had appeared out of nowhere, was admonishing her. 'Madam, *pa bon gete. Li pou aport ou mofinn!* You shouldn't be here! Don't you know it's bad luck? The rituals must be conducted properly, among males only, otherwise the soul won't be able to find its way into the afterlife and will come back to haunt the living.'

Anita ignored him and continued staring at the corpse being ravaged by the hungry flames. The great blaze, immolating everything. A piece of burning debris loosened itself and was whipped from the fire by a sudden gust of wind. Anita stood, frozen, as the chunk of wood windmilled past her. She coughed and bent over as smoke billowed into her eyes, and reluctantly staggered backwards. The wind picked up and fanned the flames, carrying a rain of sparks like a display of fireworks.

'*Mo finn dir ou napa gete!*' the man insisted.

Anita was sufficiently annoyed by his hectoring tone to tell him to mind his own business before submerging herself back in the darkness of the shadows.

'A non-believer with no respect for the dead!' the man muttered under his breath, before making a big show of pulling phlegm up his throat and spitting it loudly in the courtyard. '*Tchi, tchi, pagli!*'

The man proceeded to sweep the decaying leaves into a pyramid-shaped pile, leaving them to rot until they could be buried as compost to feed the seedlings that would sprout new life from the earth. He ignored Anita this time and retreated into the shade. He was darkness within the darkness. His pointy face reminded her of an angry mongoose.

Anita was aware that according to Hindu traditions, the mukhagni should only be witnessed by the male relatives of the deceased, but Anita was not afraid of death.

The first time she had seen a dead body, she was about seven. It was at the funeral of her aunt, who had died of suicide. Anita could still remember every detail: the fleas angrily circling the open casket, the body on full display in the middle of the crammed living room, the lingering smell of death. No amount of fresh flowers or incense could dispel the stench of decomposition in the heat. The dead woman's swollen lips and throat had turned almost black from the bottles of insecticide she had gulped in despair, hoping for respite. It looked as if the insidious liquid had not only taken her life but also dissolved the skin while it wound its way into her tender stomach.

To this day, despite Anita's probing, she still did not know the full story. Ma, still hobbled by grief for her younger sibling, refused to delve into the past. Whatever had really happened, Anita knew it was an ugly story that the family preferred to keep buried.

When relatives and neighbours had come to pay their respects to the dead woman and take part in the funeral rituals, an uncle whose penchant for cheap rum had got the better of him was too drunk that day to understand what had happened. He tottered among the crowd, dishevelled, barely able to stand up straight let alone string together intelligible words without slurring. He finally collapsed in a drunken stupor on a nearby rattan chair with his flies undone, causing the sea of faces to warp with distaste. A murmur of shock went around the crowd as they witnessed him urinate on his khaki trousers in full view of the mourners, who were already sick with grief. Two male relatives quickly materialized to rouse the uncle out of his slumber and carry him to his bed, while another rushed to get a bucket of water to mop up the puddle of urine. Some of the women had the presence of mind to chase away the children, but it was too late. Anita and her young cousins had witnessed the dead being upstaged by the living.

A thrill of repulsion went through Anita as the strong stench of burning flesh hit her. The unsettling smell of death drove her to cover her mouth and retch. Unable to bear the nauseating odour any longer, she turned around and left as the chief mourner started the kapal kriya, the ritual of piercing the burning skull with a stave to set free the spirit of the deceased to leave this world behind and enter the unknown, to guide its wandering spirit. To find the right way. To embrace life after death.

Treading on a trail of wilting flowers left by the cortège, Anita navigated her way through a cluster of people meandering past until she was back on the main road. A few minutes later, she boarded the next bus heading towards the coast. Sandwiched between two factory workers about to clock on to their morning shift, Anita caught a glimpse of the sea. As the bus left the village behind, she could see the expanse of blue at the bottom of the cane fields, beckoning her, calling her, ready to embrace her, inviting her to immerse herself in the lagoon. To surrender herself completely, release herself from the sickly smell of death that lingered on. To become one with the ocean.

That night, lying on her back in total darkness, Anita could still hear the funeral mantra being chanted above the crackling noise of burning firewood. The scorching flames were approaching her. Luring her in. Finding her in her sleep. Whispering her name, Anita Ram, in her ears. She could not escape. Her insides were ablaze, as if she had swallowed big gulps of fire. The taste of burning ashes was in her mouth, along with the chant of death. Repeated echoes in her head whirled in a fiery tornado, getting louder and louder until the voices woke her up. An internal stampede. Like the playing of a frenzied drum only she could hear.

> *Anita, Ram naam satya hai. Anita, Ram naam satya*
> *hai. Anita, Ram naam satya hai.*
> *Ram. Ram. Ram naam satya hai.*
> *Anita Ram. Anita Ram. Anita Ram.*
> *Anita. Ram.*
> *Anita.*

5

Ma was bustling about in the stuffy kitchen, clanging pots and pans. She wiped her messy hands on a dirty rag that looked like a butcher's apron and went to turn on the fire. When the purple light flickered into life, she placed a blackened karay on the stove. It was only then that she noticed her daughter's puzzled look at the bloody mess.

'It's Sunday. Your sister's coming to visit.' Ma rubbed the sweat off her brow with the back of her hand.

'Oh, I didn't realize.' Anita fell silent. She took in the lumps of red on the plate. She should have known.

'This would be a good time to talk to her.' Ma turned towards the sink to wash a couple of fresh green chillies from the garden. She turned off the tap and dried her hands on a tea towel. 'I'm making her favourite dish. I went to the bazaar really early yesterday to buy fresh goat meat. You know how much she likes a traditional goat curry.'

As if Anita could forget the incident that had put her off red meat for good.

Once a year the family sacrificed a goat, a tradition they staunchly adhered to. It was an ancient Hindu ritual that went all the way back to their forebears, who had travelled to Mauritius from Mother India. At the start of every new year, just as the gods and the ancestors' souls had to be commemorated, the hungry ghosts and powerful demons also had to be placated. According to traditional beliefs, the ritual, if conducted properly, would not only confer redemption for all the wrongs committed during the preceding year, but would also be a benediction for a propitious one ahead. The relatives would club together to purchase a kid goat – it was cheaper to buy them young – which they would fatten up so it was fully grown in time for the service.

As he grew older and more fragile, Dada, Anita's paternal grandfather, entrusted this ancestral custom to his eldest son. During the days preceding the ceremonial slaughter, the animal would be kept on a tight leash and fed several times a day. Its growth would be closely monitored in anticipation of the family feast to mark the event.

One year, unable to bear the young animal's plaintive cries after a particularly bad night, Anita tiptoed out of the house in her cotton nightie. In semi-darkness she managed to cross the acacia hedge leading to her dada's property. From somewhere far away, a dog barked at the spirits of the dead that were said to loom in the strange limbo between the living and the dead.

Anita let the laments, and the stench of the barn, guide her to the distressed animal. Once in front of the shed, she tentatively reached for the handle and pulled. It shrieked, metal grinding against metal. As she opened the heavy latch, she was hit by a pungent odour and tried to hold her breath as long as possible. When she finally inhaled, the air stank of rancid faeces, urine and rotting vegetables. Her flip-flops slipped on something soft and wet and she quickly wiped it off with some hay stored in a nearby jute sack. The goat was frantically moving about in the corner. The early-morning light shining through the small window reflected dimly on the animal's dirty pelt. There were dry patches where its fur, tangled with droppings, was stuck together in messy lumps.

She reached out for the goat, and even in the shadows she could see the fright in its eyes as it began to bleat and kick. 'Shush, ti kabri. Pa bizin to gagn per,' Anita whispered into the agitated animal's ears as it desperately pulled at the rope and skittered about in the small shed. She responded by gently stroking its grimy fur, which was warm under her touch. The colour of her fingers blended into the short pelt, which smelled like a carpet that hadn't been washed in years. The goat calmed down as it eventually realized her presence wasn't a threat.

Before losing courage, Anita reached for the wooden shelf where Dada's tools were stored. She quickly located the old sabre his own father had given him the first day he had accompanied him to the fields to cut sugar cane. Dada had only been five when he started helping his father on the plantation, earning a few sous that went a long way towards feeding the family.

The goat bleated nervously, shaking its head from side to side. With one hand steadying the animal and the sharp blade in another, Anita cut the cord that tied the poor creature to a metal post. 'Shush,' she told it.

Using both hands, she quietly led the animal out of the barn, out of the darkness, into the first light of dawn. By then the goat knew she was its saviour and followed her a few metres away from the shed. Then it gave a final stomp of its hooves before leaping into the fields towards the Corps de Garde.

'Salam, ti kabri! Now you don't have to please any man's belly. You're free. Go, ti kabri, go!'

Just before walking back to the house, Anita heard a familiar snort behind her. She went cold despite the December heat. She turned around to face her sister loitering in the shadows. When she saw the glee in her sibling's eyes, she knew exactly what was coming.

The sleuth ran back to the house to tell on Anita just as the household began to wake. Betrayed by her own flesh and blood. It was clear who would have to pay for the loss of the long-awaited, much-prized goat.

Slowly Chacha, her uncle, took off his leather belt, roughly grabbed hold of Anita's arms and turned her around to face the grungy terrace wall. With her small figure bent over the back of a metal chair, she grabbed on to the headrest as tightly as she could. She tried so hard not to flinch at every slap of the belt, which made her knuckles turn as pale as dried cement. Even more painful, though, was having to watch the slaughter of the replacement goat, which Ma had to pay for to make amends for her daughter's behaviour.

Chacha's belt buckle left red zigzags on Anita's flesh, but at least her skin did not burst open like the goat's. She kept her head high in defiance as she soundlessly took in the lashing, jaw clenched, knowing Didi was watching the scene from her hiding place. The last thing Anita wanted was to give her sister any additional satisfaction.

Later that day, from her small bedroom window overlooking the back garden, Anita heard the newly purchased goat's cries as it was dragged from the barn with a tight noose around its neck. The wretched animal had sensed its fate and tried to resist by pulling back on the cord, desperately trying to shrug it off, holding on to its precarious young life for as long as possible. Chacha grabbed the goat by the scruff of its neck. He then straddled the creature with his arm under its jaw, using excessive force to wrestle it until the animal's knees finally buckled. Its head was pinned down between two thick bamboo poles: a makeshift guillotine. A slit. The goat let out a final bleat as its head fell forward to kiss goodbye to an earth filled with blood.

When Chacha stopped to wipe his bushy brows, he left a streak of red on his forehead. A glistening tikka of blood that made his shiny, round face look incongruous. Through her uncle's half-open mouth, Anita glimpsed his knife-sharp teeth as he brandished a victorious smile at the baying crowd of relatives who had gathered to watch the ceremonial slaughter.

Chacha tied a rope around the dead animal's ankles and hung it from a branch of a longan tree. The goat's head, red with fresh blood, dripped into a steel lamok, its soft eyes still wet.

The relatives made sure the animal bled until there was nothing left. Every single drop was collected. Once the appropriate portions had been served as offerings to the gods and the ancestral spirits known as pretas, the remaining blood would be dished out to the family as blood curry, the famous kari disan.

Chacha, the eldest son, had completed his task, and it was time for the rest of the kinfolk to cut open the goat, starting with the legs and then the stomach. The goat was now upside down and inside out, dripping with slime.

Anita covered her mouth to stop herself retching. It was unsettling to watch how easily her family pulled the skin back, as if they were peeling a banana.

After they had ripped off the pelt, her relatives went for the stomach. 'Pull!' they shouted. The men's groping hands reached into the slippery insides, still soft and warm. They used their grubby fingers to grab whatever they could find, oblivious to the gunge and foul smell. Skinned and hollowed out, the dead animal would sway gently from the branch as Anita's hovering aunties waved away the flies circling its pink carcass.

As soon as the sun went down, the family had gathered around for the long-awaited feast. Anita could still remember how she had sat on a cushioned stool by herself, her lower back still sore. No one had deigned to speak to her as she toyed with a greasy puri and tamarind chutney, counting the hours until she could finally return to her friends: the foreign yet familiar characters in the novels she devoured that enabled her to leave the confines of her life and live vicariously, if only for a few hours. Shifting on her stool, she had become acutely aware of how she was being sneered at by her cousins as they heartily dug into their curry. Decades later, echoes of their laughter still resonated in Anita's ears. Nothing could drown out the malicious sounds of their mirth.

'She's always been a bit of a loner, that one.' Snippets of conversation had floated by to taunt her. The most vicious jeer had come from the moon-faced Gitanjali, by far the loudest, of whom her sister had been in awe – and still was, for reasons Anita had never understood. Perhaps their similar traits and closeness in age had bonded them. Gitanjali's parents had named her after Rabindranath Tagore's collection of devotional poems. This, they hoped, would lead their daughter to enlightenment. But their aspirations had been in vain. The last she'd heard, Gitanjali was addicted to drugs and living in Australia with her husband, a surly Swedish sect worshipper, and their brood of rowdy boys. When Anita had received a Facebook request from her, she browsed Gitanjali's family photos and then deleted the request with a shudder. Anita wanted nothing to do with the bullies from her past.

Feigning indifference, Anita had pretended not to hear her kin gossip as they chewed, dribbled and slurped the rest of the dead goat, washed down with copious amounts of tepid Coke and cheap rum. Like scavengers.

The animal's dewy eyes would not leave Anita's memory. The image haunted her as if she were the one who had slaughtered it.

The puri and tamarind chutney were silt in her gut. Didi watched her younger sister as the latter gagged, fighting the urge to vomit, but it was too late. A thick gloop erupted from her mouth. She caught a glimpse of gleefulness in Didi's eyes when the acrid smell of the vomit on her plate made her run to the bathroom. It was the same expression her older sibling had whenever Ma told her not to be mean to her sister. 'I was only playing with her, Ma!' Didi would say, smiling sweetly at her mother while brushing her hand across her forehead to smooth her greasy fringe. Anita wished she could have thrown the yellowy puke over Didi's head to wipe the smugness off her face.

That night, alone in bed, Anita had cried her heart and lungs out. She was half asleep by the time she sensed a presence in her room and heard the unsettling sound of a leather belt unbuckling in the silence. Gripped by groping hands as stiff as a goat's hooves that squeezed and pressed too hard, her young body was forced to kneel under a disgusting stink of rum, sweat and stale goat. A heavy, furry paunch pressed down on her, dripping its sticky slime all over her body. Had the animal come to punish Anita in her sleep?

Anita was abruptly brought back to the present by the thud of tender meat being hacked. Ma was slicing the congealed blood, pieces of meat and giblets and throwing them into the blackened pot, which sizzled and spat as the mixture thickened into clots as dark as cast iron. Her own body sticky with sweat and vapour, Anita covered her mouth and, once again, felt bile rise in her throat. She dashed out of the overheated kitchen to throw up in the bathroom.

'Don't bother waiting for me for lunch. I'll be home late.'

'Please, Anita! Stay and meet with your sister! You really should talk to her.'

But Anita was already out of the house, gasping for fresh air. She knew the stagnant smell of goat would linger for days, no matter how many fresh herbs and how much home-made ground masala Ma tossed into it. Goat intestine curry was something Anita would never be able to stomach.

6

The heat in the bus was almost unbearable as it jerked and lurched through streets lined with sugar cane plantations. Anita sat in a daze, looking over the fields and the horizon which melted into the sea. Her T-shirt clung to her body. She was glad when the bus reached Rivière Noire and she could finally step out of the rattling vehicle. Once outside, she could feel the heat of the pavement through the soles of her sandals, and she looked for shade at every step.

At the beach Anita threw her bag on the sand, peeled off her clothes and ran towards the sea. The beach was practically deserted. She dipped her hands in the water to cool off her neck and face, tasting its saltiness in her mouth, before wading into the ocean. The lagoon was as welcoming as a soothing bath on a winter's day. She liked the way the water formed gentle ripples around her, the fact that someone so insignificant could still leave a trace in the vast ocean.

After her swim, Anita spread her towel on the soft white sand. Lulled by the sounds of the receding waves, she offered her body to the sun, letting its warmth caress her.

At home, going through her old things, she had found a few items of clothing she could still fit into, including a slightly faded red bathing suit she had worn in her early twenties. Stress had caused her to shed a couple of kilos.

Anita moved to sit under the shade of a tree and picked up a book from her bag. Books were her only indulgence so far. To dive into one plot after another made her forget her own grief. Losing herself in the words of her old friends – Baudelaire, Sand, Molière, Flaubert, Toulet, Cabon, Pagnol, Fanchette, Maupassant, Masson – brought instant comfort. It was strange to think that these dead writers felt more alive than the living.

A shadow fell across her book. She looked up to find the little girl from her previous encounter, along with an older Indo-Mauritian woman who appeared to be her nanny, armed with a pile of toys, standing in front of her.

'Hello, Anita,' the child greeted her.

'Hello, Maya. Lovely to see you! And what a pretty dress you're wearing. With matching hair clips!'

A tiny dimple appeared on each side of the little girl's face. 'My Mama got it for me,' she said proudly.

'Where is your Mama?' asked Anita, carefully avoiding the nanny's eyes.

'In the Arbeit. She is working,' the little girl answered.

'And where does she work?'

'In an office. My Papa also works in an office. He is an artefact.'

'An artefact? Are you sure?' Anita suppressed a smile.

'Yes, he draws houses and buildings.'

'Ah! You mean an architect?'

Maya nodded and picked up Anita's book from the sand. 'And what are you reading?' She peered curiously at the cover. 'Is it a fairy tale?'

'Not quite. It's a story about a woman called Devina.'

'Your book doesn't have any pictures?' the little girl asked, slightly perplexed after staring, uncomprehending, at a couple of pages.

'No, I'm afraid it's not a picture book.' Anita shrugged apologetically.

'Warum? Why?'

'Novels don't usually have pictures.'

'And does the woman live happily ever after?'

'Unfortunately, not all stories end happily, Maya. The sooner you know this, the better!' Anita answered abruptly, unthinking, before snatching the book back. Instantly she was filled with remorse. Maya's bottom lip began to wobble as if she was about to cry, but to Anita's relief she didn't.

'Would you like to play with me? Mein Papa is also working in his Arbeit.' The little girl looked at her pleadingly, obviously desperate for new company. When the girl extended her hand, Anita caught the warm little fingers in her grip and felt her insides melt. She wanted to keep holding on, to moor herself.

'Of course! I'd love to. Here, bring me your bucket and spade.' Anita patted the sand next to her, eager to make amends for her earlier bluntness. The child's face lit up at the prospect of an impromptu play date.

Once they had built an elaborate sandcastle boasting forts festooned with seaweed and shells, and much to Maya's delight, Anita invited the little girl and her nanny to share her modest lunch. Ma had made plain cheddar pain maison sandwiches and filled a container with semi-ripe mango slices from the garden. They sat companionably, the three of them watching the distant boats ferrying groups of excited tourists to the nearby islet.

After some gentle probing, Anita found out that Maya was half Mauritian, half German. The girl lived in a nearby bungalow on the beach, near the bay of Tamarin. That was about all the information she could extract from the little girl's reticent nanny.

Maya was busy munching on a piece of bread when she spotted her father from a distance. 'Look! It's Papa,' she said, beaming. Discarding her sandwich, she ran towards her dad, who effortlessly picked her up and swirled her around before putting her down again. When Maya finally stopped giggling, she pointed at their picnic. '*Komm, Papa, setz dich zu uns*. Please come!' she said as she tugged him towards Anita and the nanny.

'Hallo. I'm Sven Steinacher.' The man held out his hand formally. He spoke clearly but with a distinct accent similar to Maya's, although the child's twang was subtler. He looked a few years older than Anita, probably late forties. His messy dark hair was streaked with silver. His eyes were the same colour as marlin fresh out of water, a combination of metallic blue and grey. He wasn't good-looking in a classical sense, yet his face was somehow pleasing.

Anita got up and shook Sven's hand, filling his palms with tiny particles of sand. 'I'm Anita… Anita Ram. Nice to meet you.' She rushed the last part of the sentence, afraid of revealing too much too soon. Although she was technically still married, it would have felt inappropriate to use Paul's surname.

'Maya's been talking a lot about you. I hope she hasn't been pestering you too much.' Sven smiled apologetically as he reached down to hold his daughter's pudgy hand. He looked almost giantlike next to her tiny figure.

'She's an adorable girl. A real darling,' she assured him with a smile. 'You and your wife must be very proud of her.'

Sven picked up Maya's flowery yellow hat, which was half buried in the sand. 'Maya said you're on holiday?' He shook off the sand and dropped the hat into the little girl's bucket.

'Sort of. I'm on sabbatical,' Anita replied vaguely, rubbing one arm with the other.

'So you're a teacher?'

'No. I'm not much of anything at the moment.'

'Really.' She was unable to read the *really*. Dismissive? Disappointed? Intrigued?

'Are you staying in Rivière Noire?'

'No. Palma, near the Medine Sugar Estate.' She looked up; he was a good few inches taller than her. Near his left eye he had a scar which ran across the arch of his thick eyebrow. It looked as if his brow had been split in two towards the end. She tried not to stare at it.

'Ach so. I hope you are enjoying your visit?'

She shrugged and looked away at the horizon as she absent-mindedly tucked a strand of hair behind her ear.

Sensing Anita's reluctance to elaborate further, Sven started picking up Maya's toys from the sand. 'It's time to go home, Fräulein.'

'*Bitte, nein* –' Maya began to protest, but her dad finally managed to cajole her with a promise of an ice lolly after dinner. 'Bye. *Bis Morgen!*' shouted Maya in her cheerful sing-song voice.

'See you tomorrow.' Anita waved back as she watched father and daughter walk back hand in hand followed by the nanny, towards the bay. She let her toes sink into the soft warm sand while listening to the lapping of the waves. The late-afternoon sun was beginning to set on the horizon, casting a timid glow on the glimmering lagoon. Staring at the vast expanse of sea ahead of her, she became acutely aware of the geographical confinement of the island, lost in the middle of the Indian Ocean.

A few fishermen were still on the beach, cleaning and weighing their catch of the day. Everywhere she looked, people were moving about with a sense of purpose. Anita felt a sudden emptiness as she watched Maya and her father stroll back towards their beach house, stopping briefly at the rocks to look in the tide pools. She imagined the meal they would share as a family in the intimacy of their home. The silly stories Maya would tell her parents, stories which would make them laugh at dinner time over a glass of chilled white wine.

Anita was hit by a pang of jealously as she thought of her early years with Paul. After the wedding, they'd both desperately wanted children. They made sure the three-bedroom Victorian terrace they bought was big enough for at least two children, and close enough to nurseries and playgrounds.

Every month, she used to dread her period, hating that sudden rush of unwelcome blood down her inner thigh or waking up to bloody stains on their pristine Egyptian cotton sheets. The rusty marks were a blatant reminder that her body was incapable of nurturing life. The egg, yet again, simply refused to embed itself in her womb.

A sense of despondency washed over Anita as she recalled her longing for children of her own. She had desperately wanted to conceive, but after a few years of fruitless trying, it was finally confirmed: she could not be a mother; could not hold her newborn in her arms, inhale her baby's sweet milky scent, watch her children grow, kiss their cheeks warm with sleep. Read them stories. Hug them goodnight.

With time, they stopped referring to the spare room as the nursery, especially after the failed attempts at IVF, unproductive endeavours which had to be abandoned.

She eventually moved an escritoire into the room, one she had stumbled upon at a weekend flea market, and spent hours there hunched over thick piles of legal documents, meticulously reviewing and editing them clause by clause. It was around the time Paul was being considered for partnership at his firm. So they both channelled their disappointment into furthering their careers, although this seemed to work much faster for him. It seemed to her there was an obvious reason for this.

When she had voiced her frustrations to Paul one evening over dinner, he tried to console her with what he clearly saw as words of wisdom. He told her to be patient, seemingly oblivious to the implications as she watched her white female colleagues – with less experience and fewer qualifications – take on more prominent roles within the law firm. It was like watching streams become rivers that gushed past her while she remained in shallow waters, stagnating.

Soon, the distant figures of Maya and her father could no longer be seen from the shore. Anita turned away. She picked up a piece of driftwood half buried in the sand, pared down and bleached by the sea, and reburied it even deeper. Slowly, she gathered her possessions from the sand and trudged back towards the bus stop, the wind blowing against her.

That night, Anita had an unsettling dream of herself and a little girl, who was wearing a white cotton dress. They were singing lullabies and whirling wildly on the beach, bathing in the light of the full moon.

'Mummy!' The girl held out her arms as she laughed, and for one brief moment there was hope as bright as a lighthouse beacon in the dark. But when Anita reached out to embrace her, the little girl disappeared. Anita ran after the child, looking for her in vain. In the moonlight, the girl had seemed a spectral figure, one she could see but not touch.

Anita woke up abruptly, covered in sweat, overcome by a feeling of melancholy. She felt she had lost someone very dear to her.

7

The next couple of days were quietly whiled away. Anita quickly found her own quiet rhythm: solitary escapades on the beach: strolling along the firm, wet, tide-ribbed sand. Her daily swims felt spiritual, ritualistic. The quasi-sacramental water seemed to enter her every cell, every particle of her body, cleansing her soul.

Most days she saw Maya accompanied by her Indo-Mauritian nanny. Although she always kept a watchful eye on her charge, the older woman kept to herself and hardly spoke. In contrast with the nanny's dourness, Maya was a bubbly four-year-old brimming with energy whose company Anita was beginning to enjoy. It was refreshing to see the world through the eyes of a child. Her insouciance and enthusiasm were slowly starting to rub off. Maya occasionally referred to her 'Mama' but, as Anita never saw the child's mother, she assumed she was busy working.

After a morning of playing and paddling in the sea with her new friend, Anita watched the little girl fall asleep to the gentle lull of the receding waves. There was a smile of contentment on Maya's face as she slept. Being with the child reminded Anita of the feelings she had once nurtured for her only niece. The memories came rushing back to her like a strong tide.

The first time she had met Nisha as a baby, she had breathed in her sweet, milky scent and lovingly traced her finger over her sleepy face in disbelief at the tiny bundle, wondering how her sister could have created such a perfect little creature. Her broderie anglaise minidress with its matching culottes and drawstring hat were like clothes made for a porcelain doll. In hindsight, she had seemed so innocent and vulnerable as Anita held her in her arms. And yet it was uncanny how, eighteen years later, the roles had reversed: it was Anita who now felt like a fragile porcelain doll.

Distant scenes of Nisha as a child kept floating in and out of her mind. Anita remembered cradling her baby niece against her chest. One by one she would kiss her tiny eyes which didn't yet have brows, humming the same lullabies Ma used to sing to her as a child before she drifted off to sleep. Songs every Mauritian child learned by rote in childhood.

> *Ki pase la?*
> *Marsan dile*
> *Ki dile?*
> *Dile kaye*
> *Ki kaye?*
> *Kaye devwar*
> *Ki devwar?*
> *Devwar Angle*
> *Ki Angle?*
> *Angle potis...*

And as she drifted off to sleep her mother's comforting scent, a combination of sandalwood, earth and the sea, would always linger in her dreams. Ma's voice was as soft as the murmur of a bubbling brook which meandered into a river, carried away by the flows and currents that kissed the mouth of the sea before joining the ocean; a soft blanket of blue that wrapped the island like a berceau, a cradle rocked to sleep by the gentle lull of the waves.

Whenever Anita went to the bazaar, she would buy trinkets for Nisha: half a dozen glass bangles coated with a sprinkle of glitter, anklets with tiny bells that jingled whenever her niece took a few tentative steps, flowery clips for her silky black hair or a handful of candied papaya from *laboutik sinwa*, the Chinese shop.

Together they would dance to Ma's favourite Bollywood songs. Nisha was a sharp child who was always quick to imitate Anita's graceful moves as she clapped and twirled to the upbeat music blaring out of the radio.

Sometimes they would dig holes in the garden for Ma to plant neat beds of thyme, spring onions, coriander and tulsi. Anita would ask her niece to fetch the watering can or turn on the tap, and the child would immediately obey Anita with an air of importance and the joy of feeling needed.

Once, as Anita was making a fresh mango and tamarind salad, Nisha stood close behind to watch. Afterwards, to impress her parents, Nisha had replicated Anita's salad, pretending it had been her own invention and basking in their praise. Anita thought there was something strange in the way the child constantly sought her parents' approval, but she put it down to Nisha being an only child. And although her niece's misappropriation nettled her a little, she didn't think much of it at the time.

When Anita bought gold rings to put on her toes while wearing sandals, Nisha begged to have the exact same ones, which Anita was happy to provide. Wasn't imitation the sincerest form of flattery?

They used to read together, giggling while poring over picture books in Ma's kitchen, made steamy by creamy manioc slowly cooked in vanilla-infused milk with a hint of cardamom.

The aroma was so delicious that Anita wished she could eat the air. Ma would laugh at Nisha's funny pronunciation, the way her grandchild mixed up words, saying 'ti pato' instead of 'ti bato' whenever she referred to a boat. Or how she kept saying 'water-lemon' instead of 'watermelon'. Ma would smile indulgently at her only grandchild's mischievousness, like the time Nisha hid her reading glasses in the bathroom after accidentally breaking them, or when she sprayed herself with Anita's expensive perfume without permission.

A few years later, on a particularly miserable day when the clouds glided across the wet London sky like giant frothy waves, Anita found herself perusing old books during her lunch hour. Whenever she could, she would visit the antiquarian book-sellers tucked behind Covent Garden, looking for lost treasures. With a flutter of pride, she unearthed an early edition of *Alice's Adventures in Wonderland* and recognized the vintage illustration of Alice's encounter with the famous Mauritian Dodo. Holding the book reverently in her hands, she inhaled the familiar musty smell of old paper. As the pictures beckoned her in, she lovingly turned the yellowing pages and was immediately transported back to her childhood. Delighted to have stumbled upon this rare gem, she happily handed over a fair amount of cash to give the treasured book to her niece as a birthday present. When Anita later called, Nisha dutifully thanked her aunt. However, before putting down the receiver, she overheard Didi's nasal voice in the background. 'She earns good money in London and buys her only niece a second-hand gift for her birthday!' Anita felt her heart plummet.

A couple of years later, when Anita heard that Nisha was planning to redecorate her bedroom, she sent her a glossy coffee table book on the basics of interior design and feng shui, with which the young girl quickly became enthralled. She later found out that Didi had complained to her husband: 'I don't want her to indoctrinate our daughter with her yin and yang ideas!' she had barked.

Every year, for Diwali, Anita sent money over to her niece. Whenever she called, she would always enquire about her school and friends, and sometimes liked to think of herself as the cool aunt from London who bought Nisha the latest fashion magazines, her first make-up kit and even her first bra from Marks & Spencer. Anita had enjoyed the feeling of conspiracy between the two of them whenever Nisha had turned to her aunt for advice. In return, she had showered the girl with all her love and affection, for it made her feel, if only fleetingly, like the mother she would never be.

Not once did she think of her protégée as a threat.

8

Tired of building sandcastles, Anita and Maya decided to create a bracelet from the shells and corals they had collected earlier on the beach. After selecting a few colourful pieces with holes, they were carefully strung on a rubber band from Anita's hair.

Anita watched Maya concentrate on her task as if nothing were more important in the world and envied the little girl's patience. When Maya finished beading, she reverently handed the bracelet to Anita. 'There. It's for you, Anita.' The child articulated every syllable of her name clearly: A-Ni-Ta. Hearing her name like that, with such different emphasis, left Anita feeling, not unpleasantly, as if she had become a different person.

'Well, thank you very much, Maya. I shall treasure it always.' Anita laughed as she dramatically held the bracelet to her heart for effect. She couldn't remember the last time she had laughed. It felt odd and yet refreshing at the same time. It struck Anita that she could truly be herself in the presence of the child, who posed no threat and didn't seem to want anything from her.

'You have to wear it. Warte! Let me help you.' Maya helped Anita tie the bracelet carefully around her wrist. 'Wunderschön! Jolie!' She took a step back to admire her chef-d'œuvre, clapping her small hands in delight.

Anita sensed that they were being watched, and realized Sven was standing a few yards away. He waved when she looked up. She smiled back, feeling self-conscious. 'Maya. Your Papa is here,' she announced.

'*Papa. Schnell. Bitte!*' The child jumped up and sprang towards Sven. 'You must come and see what we made!'

'Let me guess. You built another sea palace for the baby crabs to live in?' he asked teasingly.

'Nein! No. *Bitte komm!*' she urged him.

When her dad reached them, Maya grabbed hold of Anita's hand and placed it in Sven's so he could admire their make-shift bracelet. Anita's body tensed at this unexpected bout of intimacy. Not wishing to disappoint Maya, she let Sven take her hand as he contemplated the assortment of shells strung together.

His hand felt disconcertingly soft for a man's. He was stand-ing close enough for her to feel his breath on her salty skin, which minutes before had been caressed by the waves. 'Pretty,' he finally said, presumably referring to the bracelet but looking at Anita. He let go of her hand. She self-consciously fiddled with the shells on her wrist.

'Come. We have to go, Fräulein. Your Mama will be here soon.' Sven started gathering the toys lying on the sand. 'She's taking you to her place in Albion this weekend. Remember?' Anita looked up, perplexed. Sven held her gaze for slightly longer than necessary. And it finally dawned upon her that Maya was not living with her mother.

She waved them goodbye as he effortlessly lifted Maya onto his shoulders. A translucent white light embraced them as they strolled back towards Tamarin Bay. Looking at the sea spread before her, Anita suddenly felt like a grain of sand in front of its sheer immensity.

9

The sky was cloudy and the air filled with a damp petrichor scent. Anita was starting to feel restless as the most painful memories of her former life in England flooded back to taunt her. For want of something better to do than staring out of the window and reminiscing about her failed marriage, she decided to sort out her old bedroom.

Armed with an array of carrier bags and empty cardboard boxes, she meticulously went through her former belongings. She pulled out an old necklace from a box. The gold plate had turned almost green with grit and time, tarnished with something impossible to remove. Anita threw it away, together with the tacky jewellery box full of cheap necklaces tangled around broken glass bangles and decade-old, now odourless Avon bottles, presents from relatives living in England.

She cleared the stacks from the bulging shelves and pulled drawers from their runners, emptying their useless contents into the bags, wiping them clean.

One by one, she went through her old school things, meeting each book with a sense of reunion, like seeing a long-lost friend, before packing them in neatly labelled boxes to give away to charity. She decluttered an assortment of clothes and bric-a-brac from her former life.

At some point Ma joined her, and they worked together in companionable silence, listening to the sounds of dense tropical rain against the shaky windowpanes.

'Should we be getting rid of all this?' Ma wondered as she lovingly folded stacks of her daughter's clothes.

Anita shrugged. 'I'll never use these things again, so I might as well give them away.' She was holding a Banarasi sari wrapped in faded sheets of newspaper, with little white balls of naphthalene to protect against moths. Their smell filled her nostrils.

'We should keep this one,' Ma said as she stroked an Indian silk dress hanging in the wardrobe alongside a pair of matching drawstring trousers with silver embroidery. From the corner of her eye, Anita caught Ma discreetly rubbing her eyes with the loose end of her sari. 'Your father and I bought it for you in Mumbai. It was during our last trip in India.'

When her mother spoke again, her voice was quieter, lost in the fog of memory or pain, with a faraway look in her eyes whenever she spoke of her late spouse. He might not have been the husband she had wished for, but she had remained loyal and devoted until the end, a good Hindu wife. Ma's endurance and ability to put up with her late husband's weaknesses was the epitome of Mauritian women's strength. And who cared if the women were occasionally shoved around? It had been expected of her, and of all the women who had come before her. Ma had been brought up to overlook her husband's indiscretions and simply accept her fate. There were rumours that he had fathered a number of children with other women, including one of Anita's teachers, but as long as he provided for his wife and their daughters the relatives kept quiet. Women of Ma's generation did not talk about things that would bring shame to the family. Instead, they hid behind the facade of a good, prayer-loving Mauritian Hindu family. They were too afraid of family dishonour. It was better to pretend than to upset the status quo. Who would want to be the one responsible for disturbing the peace? Religious fasts were obeyed, hefty donations made to temples and priests, gods worshipped and holy rituals adhered to. As long as the night remained silent, what happened within the walls of respectable Mauritian homes was irrelevant.

Ma had never got over her husband's sudden departure. He had left home early, promising to be back by three o'clock to drop off Anita at the Alliance française for her French classes. But on that tragic day, Pa didn't even make it to work. He died instantly behind the wheel after a lorry cut across his path. At least that was the official version, put about to save face.

His death had been hard on Anita, then aged eight, too young to have a father taken away from her. Wouldn't his grief at leaving his family behind have been just as intense, despite all his flaws? She wondered if the dying had such thoughts on the threshold to another world.

She recalled overhearing Ma as she had tearfully told friends and relatives that the worst part was clearing his things away, wiping the traces of his existence from this life. 'That's when it finally hits you that he won't be coming back. Never again.' Ma loved him more in death than she ever had in life. It was strange how the living deferred to the dead, in awe of those departed, especially those who left too soon.

At the funeral, it was shocking for young Anita to see her mother crumble and weep like a child. Her body had shaken as she had let out pained, keening wails, ululations of grief that left permanent dark shadows beneath her eyes and pale lines alongside her mouth. Her whole demeanour had been pulled down in mourning. When Anita looked into her mother's eyes, for a long time she could see only sadness.

Her sister was already a young adult when Pa died. Sick with grief, she hysterically kicked and shouted at Anita, her face twisted in anger. 'If it wasn't for your stupid French tuition, Pa wouldn't have had to go to work so early! Now I have to stop my training and start working.'

Overcome with guilt, Anita had tried to make herself as insignificant as possible so as not to cause further grief. She learned how to clam up, how to make herself scarce and avoid drawing attention to herself.

A year later, her sister met her prospective husband at the ministry where she worked as an official, thanks to a well-connected uncle who had managed to pull some strings. Connections were vital in bagging a government post – with the help of some baksheesh, naturally.

After Didi's wedding, Anita was secretly relieved when her sister moved to the north of the island to join her husband's family, leaving Ma and Anita to live companionably in a house devoid of rivalry and tension. Her mother was finally free to give her undivided attention to her youngest daughter without having to feel guilty.

Didi had an irritating sense of entitlement, as if the world owed her everything simply for being the firstborn. Whenever she visited, her presence, however brief, always managed to interrupt the equilibrium in the house. Her bimonthly visits for Sunday lunch felt like a duty, equal parts frustration and triumph, as she reminded Ma to pay the bills, as she bustled about the living room sorting out letters and hectoring Ma for not filing them. Didi would sigh, a long, slow exhalation that seemed to make the air move differently in the room. During Anita's absence, she had even managed to inveigle Ma into signing the proxy documents over to her, giving her carte blanche to single-handedly 'manage' their late father's property. 'Just some routine paperwork I don't want to bother you with,' she had casually informed Ma. It later turned out that she had made a transfer to her private bank account to acquire a generous plot of land near the beach, thereby wiping out most of Pa's legacy. Didi failed to disclose the full extent of the transaction to Ma, or to inform her younger sibling, who was also legally entitled to a share of their late father's estate. Transparency had never been her sister's forte, especially when she felt something should be hers. Self-righteous Didi had a cunning way of making the decisions for everyone.

After chiding Ma, her sister would then proceed to inspect Anita's bedroom and interrogate her about school, demanding to see her homework and belittling her achievements whenever she could. Every time she left Ma and Anita, it would be with discernible smugness and satisfaction on her face. In light of her sister's constant nagging, Anita had, in those days, felt sorry for her brother-in-law and only niece.

When Anita, brimming with pride, had called Didi to tell her she had won a scholarship to study in England, her sister had responded coolly. 'Oh, good for you!' she said, half-congratulating her younger sibling. 'And who's going to look after Ma now you're leaving her? It's usually the youngest child's duty to look after her parents,' she reminded her.

Winning the scholarship was as though a luxury cruise ship had sailed into view, broadening Anita's horizon. The vessel's appearance was an invitation to embark on an exciting journey of discovery.

'You'll have to face her sooner or later, you know.'

Ma's words brought Anita back to the present. Instead of answering her mother, she looked away, pretending to be engrossed in folding a T-shirt with the print of a colourful dodo. The silence between them swelled and filled the room. A fly buzzed angrily against the windowpane.

'She's called a few times. Nisha is her only daughter.'

'Why should I? Anyway, I already told you I'm not ready.' Anita hastily thrust a stack of unwanted clothes into a bag, avoiding eye contact with her mother.

'It's not easy for your sister,' Ma added. 'Your brother-in-law is also very upset. It's understandable. You should talk with them.'

'And you think it's been easy for me?' Anita shot back more sharply than she had intended. She could feel anger welling up, rage crashing over her in a wave, dragging her with it.

'It's not your sister's fault.'

'Well, perhaps she should have done a better job raising that daughter of hers!' she retorted before lugging a couple of bags bursting with clothes into the garage.

'Anita! That's my only grandchild you're talking about! And it takes two to tango!' Ma shouted behind her.

Anita did not care to listen to the rest of her tirade and kicked open the garage door with much more force than necessary. She had never imagined it would be possible to despise one's own sister and niece the way she now did.

Fuming, she was reluctant to leave her task unfinished. She carried on alone, pausing every now and then for a tea break, going to great lengths to avoid Ma.

A few hours later, feeling satisfied with her progress, Anita eyed the few items she had decided to keep. It looked as if the room had been disembowelled, leaving behind an empty shell – something to which Anita could relate.

The hands of the clock indicated that it was past midnight when she finally collapsed onto the bed, feeling lighter, her uncombed hair damp from her recent shower. She fell asleep breathing in the lingering scent of naphthalene and mildew.

That night she had a nightmare in which her brother-in-law brandished a machete, threatening to kill Paul. 'Wait until I lay my hands on that English bastard!' he spat. In the dream, Didi was pointing her finger at Anita, jabbing it perilously close to Anita's chest, looking down at her younger sibling with rage.

'If only you had been a good wife!'

Those words kept echoing in her head until Anita felt like screaming.

The day felt flat and grey, like a dead fish, when Anita boarded an early bus to the coast. The weather was murky and humid, with the occasional bout of tropical rain. The old vehicle had prickly seats covered in a smelly material that was cold to the touch. From behind the window, which had turned opaque with condensation, she watched steam rise from the asphalt. After a while, the bus turned and trundled down through the small village of Bambous, past a girls' secondary school.

The sight of a bunch of teenage girls walking in the rain, uniforms grazing their knees, unearthed an incident from the recesses of her memory.

When Anita had attended Loreto Convent School, she was told by the nuns that as long as they were wearing school uniform, the girls had to behave in an impeccable manner that would reflect well on the establishment. One afternoon after tuition, Anita, who was then thirteen, had been walking towards the bus stop with the sleeves of her blouse rolled up almost to her shoulders. The heat was unbearable, so she crossed the road, looking for shade, until she found herself next to an acacia hedge that lined the deserted street. A lanky, bearded man, who had been observing her approach, asked her to show him her knickers. Just like that. Alarmed, she hurried to the other side of the street. When she reached the far corner, she turned and saw through a gap in the bushes that the man had his own pants down and was touching himself frantically. Disturbed by this graphic display and his fixed stare, she sprinted down the road.

The bus came to a sudden halt at Rivière Noire. Anita quickly gathered her things and jumped out of the vehicle before it took off towards the south.

Once on the shore, she watched the little pirogues that seemed to float motionless in the water. Nearby, a soaring pink pigeon took on a coral hue against the dull sky, interrupting her solitude. She trudged towards Le Morne Brabant, the mountain which rose from the peninsula at the tip of the ocean like an impressive fortress.

Riddled with dark caves and steep cliffs that were not easily accessible, Le Morne had been a hideaway for Maroons during colonial times, before slavery was abolished in 1835. The run-away slaves had hidden in its dense forest in an attempt to escape their horrific fate. Unaware of the change in law that had granted them 'freedom', and distrusting their (ex-)owners, they had continued building a community of fugitives in the depths of the mountain. A phalanx of officers had allegedly been sent to inform the Maroons of the abolition of slavery. Unable to bear the sight of a uniform-clad troop marching towards them with fierce-looking dogs in their wake, the tracked-down slaves had flung themselves off the steep cliffs. The wind howling in the mountain was said to be the eerie wailing of the Maroons as their painful deaths echoed over the ocean.

Walking along the beach, under the watchful stare of the gloomy mountain ahead, Anita thought of the men and women who had literally been driven to the edge of the cliff. She wondered how it must have felt, and how desperate they must have been, to jump off a precipice into an abyss. Maybe they had felt free at last, like kestrels plunging towards the ocean.

Anita stopped by Le Barachois arcade on her way back to Palma. There was a small cafe opposite a stall displaying colourful pareos and trinkets made of shells. Next to it was a DIY shop, where she bought light bulbs to replace the ones missing in Ma's house. Once in the shop, she couldn't resist picking up a few items to brighten her room. After spending the better part of an hour exploring different palettes, Anita settled on a soothing olive green and a light champagne. The salesperson helped her lug the cans of emulsion, a potted plant and a series of shopping bags onto a taxi.

When she got back, she found Ma quietly peeling potatoes on the terrace, surrounded by a line of geraniums of various sizes growing in recycled containers. Her mother stood up at the unusual sight of a taxi parking by the gate. 'What on earth did you buy?' she exclaimed without preamble, while the taxi driver unloaded the boot.

'Just a few things for my room.'

'So much?' Her mother took in the plant, the cans of paint and the shopping bags.

'I've decided to do it up.'

Fishing her purse out of her bag, Anita could feel Ma's disapproving glare as she handed a few hundred rupees, half of what she used to pay for a short minicab ride in London, to the driver. 'Thank you, madam, and good luck with the renovations,' he said, waving cheerfully as he gladly pocketed the change.

'I hope it didn't cost too much,' said Ma, arms folded.

'Don't worry. I still have my savings,' Anita replied, tossing her wallet back into her bag before zipping it shut in one brusque movement. She had hardly splurged on anything lately. After Paul's departure, she had checked her bank balance; it was healthier than she had expected.

'Your savings won't last forever, you know,' Ma cautioned.

'I've been a student before. I'm quite capable of maintaining a frugal life,' Anita replied, in an apparent non sequitur.

'Oh, I can see that,' Ma shot back, one hand on her ample hip.

Ignoring Ma's comment, Anita lifted a bag from the floor, struggling slightly under its weight.

'Are you planning to do this on your own?'

Anita nodded. 'It's not a big deal to paint a couple of walls. I've done it before.' She shifted the weight of the bag she was carrying.

'You should ask Sailesh the gardener to help you. He usually comes twice a week,' her mother said, more gently.

'Thanks. But I'd much rather not rely on anyone,' Anita snapped back. She walked into the house and kicked open the bedroom door with her foot.

As Anita emptied the shopping bags, it struck her that only six months ago she had been busy redecorating the spare room to accommodate her special guest from Mauritius – her sister's eighteen-year-old daughter, whose studies she had generously sponsored. Whom she had warmly welcomed into her London home and showered with love and affection, making sure her niece would not have to go through what she had experienced to survive in England. She had protected her to soften the blows of displacement, given her a home from home. But how naive she had been.

It was hot and sticky outside. Leaving the house was like walking into a furnace. When Anita pulled the curtains to block out the sunlight, she was distracted by loud humming. Looking up, she got carried away staring at the Air Mauritius plane cutting through the cloudless ether, its red and white logo set against the clear blue sky.

The first time Anita had ever set foot on a plane was the day she had left Mauritius all those years ago. A teenager barely out of school, doted on by a devout mother, there was no way she could have been prepared for the next episode of her life.

Ma accompanied her to the airport on that rainy day in July. 'Promise me you'll write every week, beti.'

Anita avoided looking at her mother's pinched lips and her creased sari, draped too short. She put on a brave face for her mother's sake. 'Don't worry about me. I'll be fine.'

Soon she would be unpacking her few things in a cold, sterile room on the other side of the world. A couple of her favourite books. A pair of jeans and two jumpers bought cheaply from a factory seconds shop in Floréal. A denim skirt, a long cardigan, a silky Indian blouse and a pashmina impregnated with the scent of sandalwood. Ma had provided her with a supply of vanilla tea, some dry manioc biscuits and a few packets of Kraft cheddar for emergencies. In her thick jumper, she had carefully wrapped a small mason jar filled with pure white sand and some cowrie shells. She desperately needed to carry a little bit of her island with her. A portable home. Cowrie shells were supposed to bring good luck, and she needed all the luck possible for her new life ahead.

Taking a deep breath, Anita walked through the departures gate of Sir Seewoosagur Ramgoolam International Airport, clutching her satchel tightly for fear of losing her precious travel documents. The few neatly folded fifty-pound notes, hidden at the bottom of the bag, felt like a fortune to her. A distant quote swam up in her mind: 'If adventures will not befall a young lady in her own village, she must seek them abroad.' Never had the words of Jane Austen caused her so much distress.

As soon as Ma's receding figure disappeared, the tears finally flowed down Anita's face. She kept mopping them, but they wouldn't stop. From the plane window, she noticed the observation deck, where she imagined Ma assembled with other relatives waving goodbye to their loved ones. Her mother would stand there, watching the aircraft until it drifted out of sight into the sky. On the journey back home, Ma would sit silently, staring at the clouds above and worrying about her youngest daughter leaving the nest, wondering how she would fare out in the big world.

The machine picked up speed and Anita watched as Mauritius shrank further and further into the distance until it was nothing but a speck of dust floating in the middle of the Indian Ocean. Anita wondered when she would see it again. Having never left her small island before, she was not sure what awaited her in England.

She sat rigid in her allocated plane seat. Her feet hurt in the new closed shoes. She kicked them off, but then her temples started to throb. She tried to massage them with her eyes shut, but it made no difference. Suffering from the assault of the air conditioning, she pulled her new cardigan tightly around her, but the woolly material was itchy against her dry skin.

Unable to fight the nausea overcoming her, Anita grabbed the brown airsickness bag and retched into it. Was this some kind of premonition? After wiping her mouth with a paper napkin, she absent-mindedly flicked through the in-flight magazine. Trolleys of miniature food and drink came and went. She took a cold metal tray, but then returned the bland vegetables almost untouched. The potato dish she had toyed with tasted nothing like Ma's potatoes sautéed in her special blend of spices and a handful of sweet peas from the garden. Halfway through a Bollywood movie, she eventually managed to snatch some sleep, but not much.

Anita had a strange dream in which her Indian ancestors who had bravely crossed the treacherous Kala Pani seemed to be warning her of something lurking around the corner. If they had been able to leave their homeland more than a hundred years ago, she told herself, then why couldn't she do the same? It was a comforting thought.

Twelve hours after leaving Mauritius, Anita was awakened by the cabin crew's announcement for all passengers to remain seated and fasten their seat belts. They were about to start their descent. She sat up in her tiny seat, hair dishevelled, and stretched her numb legs as far as she could in the confined space. She took a deep breath and closed her eyes in anticipation.

The plane lurched forward as it hit the tarmac at Heathrow, finally making contact with English soil. It was hard to believe. She had made it. Great Britain. The Thames. Buckingham Palace. Big Ben. The Tower of London. Trafalgar Square. Hyde

Park. Westminster Abbey. St Paul's. Shakespeare. The Brontë sisters. Virginia Woolf. Jane Austen.

Peering out of the small window, dotted with tiny drops of rain that slowly slid down the pane, she caught a blurry first glimpse of her new life. Everything seemed to have taken a grey, foggy hue: the tarmac, the sky, the planes, the buildings, even the people.

Having left the aircraft, she dutifully followed the signs leading towards Immigration. Walking down the corridors, she crossed paths with an older woman sweeping the floor and immediately smiled at her familiar, Indian face. In return, the woman looked right through her and resumed her tedious task, lost in her own world. There was something haunting about the old woman's demeanour as she mechanically performed her duty, eyes devoid of any expression.

Anita had never felt so out of place. She waited patiently in line at the immigration desk, apprehensively clutching her brand-new passport, student visa and university papers. The other passengers looked bored. When she finally reached the counter, the immigration officer began to interrogate her.

'Where are you travelling from?'

'Mauritius.' She handed him the passport with the Mauritian coat of arms emblazoned on the glossy front cover.

'Can I see your visa?' he demanded without looking up.

Nervous, she dropped the pile of papers. The officer sighed impatiently as Anita bent down to gather the scattered documents from the carpet. Her hands started to shake when she picked them up one by one.

Someone suddenly towered above her. 'Would you please step aside to be interviewed?' As if she had a choice. 'This way.'

Quietly, she followed the officer who had materialized out of nowhere.

The white people looked away; the coloured ones had pity in their eyes.

Anita was taken to a small, windowless room with a plain table and three plastic chairs and asked to sit down. With a feeling of dread, she wondered if she would be deported before even setting foot outside the airport.

A few minutes later, two immigration officers entered the cabin and started firing questions at her. Why was she travelling to London? What was the purpose of her visit? What was she going to study? Which university? How much cash was she travelling with? What was her financial situation? Where exactly would she live? Did she have relatives in England? What did they do for a living?

Suspiciously, they examined her papers one by one before asking her to open her hand luggage. She watched as one of the men painstakingly put on gloves before going through her belongings, including her underwear. Anita could not understand what was happening. She had a perfectly valid student visa and all the right paperwork from the university. She was a bright, eighteen-year-old laureate from a 'good' family in Mauritius. Back home, she was used to the respect that her background, her family name, her neighbourhood, her education and her accent bestowed. But in England she was immediately singled out and judged according to social norms she was completely unaware of.

After what felt like an eternity spent under their scrutiny, the officers finally told Anita she could go. In a small voice devoid of any sarcasm, she thanked them, picked up her bag and left the room quietly, feeling soiled.

12

After a bumpy start on British soil, Anita tried to settle down as best she could. But a few weeks later she would suffer another ordeal, this time at the hands of someone she had put her trust in.

Anthony Beaufort, professor of property and trust law, was Oxbridge-educated, tall, articulate, and had a sense of humour as dry as the Atacama. His lectures were highly stimulating, and he seemed genuinely interested in Anita's work and enthusiasm for learning. It was shortly after half-term when he had requested a meeting to discuss her assignment on the transfer of chattels and the doctrine of acquired rights. To have Professor Beaufort as her mentor felt like a privilege. Being the diligent and eager-to-please student she was, Anita did what was asked of her. She met the professor at the assigned hour, in his dark, wood-panelled office located at the back of the building, long after her fellow students had left for the pub.

Under the pretence of praising her well-researched essay, he moved his chair closer to hers, inch by inch, until she could feel his legs almost touching her calves. He slowly crept into her personal space in the already confined office.

'I have never met anyone from Mauritius before.' He had a way of talking about Mauritius as if it were Mars. 'Are all the young ladies from your little island as exotic-looking as you?' Something languid crept into the professor's tone as he fixed his steely-blue eyes on her chest.

At that point Anita realized the balance had shifted. Unable to find a suitable answer, she mumbled something about Mauritius being a melting pot while trying to squirm away as fast as she could. But he had detained her by placing his pale hand on her tanned leg, just above the hemline of her knee-length denim skirt. Paralysed, she could only emit a nervous sound of protest.

The professor's small, hawkish eyes pierced his rimless glasses to linger on her thighs, mentally removing every single item of clothing she was wearing, until she felt naked under his leer. Young, vulnerable and defenceless.

Brandishing his stature as a shield, he held her gaze before pronouncing, pompously, that as a professor at a prestigious English university he could make her life so much easier. He left the rest of the thinly veiled threat hanging in the air that was oppressing her, preventing her from breathing. Before she could process the full implication of his words, she felt his sweaty hand slide smoothly up her skirt.

Anita was too shocked to speak or move. She felt him tower above her as he tightened his grip possessively, pinning her down. His face turned a darker shade of crimson. He was oblivious to the strangulated sounds of protest that came from somewhere deep inside her; his successive intakes of breath were short and quick. Invasive.

Anita scrambled out of Professor Beaufort's office, humiliated beyond description, desperately trying to stop her legs from shaking. Once outside, disoriented and shocked, her tears mingled with the cold English rain. Although the streets were filled with people, she had never felt more alone and insignificant in her entire life.

Back in student halls, ignoring her flatmates, she marched straight into the bathroom, locking the door firmly behind her.

She turned on the shower tap, filling the room with steam into which she wished she could evaporate. Crouched on the tiled floor, arms wrapped around her knees, she let the heat and the water pressure strafe her.

Despite washing herself repeatedly under the scalding water, scrubbing herself clean until her skin ached, the shameful smell of a humiliated woman still lingered on. It had penetrated her deeply.

The smell followed her wherever she went. It was always with her. Even in her sleep. Especially in her sleep. The scent of fear. The lingering smell of the Master. The Professor. The Oppressor.

For days, Anita couldn't drag herself out of bed. She missed her lectures as she retreated further and further underneath her duvet, letting the images beat against her like waves breaking a rock. She went back through all the sordid details, torturing herself, harbouring the masochistic belief that she had inadvertently encouraged him somehow. Was she, once again, to be blamed?

Unable to face the reflection in her mirror, she grabbed the nearest pair of scissors and chopped off her long black hair. Strands fell on the floor softly, just like her tears. She threw away all her clothes that could be construed as vaguely suggestive and resorted to wearing shapeless, baggy jeans with oversized jumpers and trainers: outfits in which she could hide, or perhaps even erase herself completely.

Whenever she could no longer ignore the whining of her stomach, she would reluctantly leave her room and venture into the common kitchen for some supermarket-brand cornflakes, which she swallowed with sour milk long past its use-by date. It was too much of an effort to make the journey across the road to the shop. Besides, what was the point of nourishing her body only to attract leeches that would slowly suck the life out of her?

After a couple of weeks, she was reminded of the stories she had heard about foreign students being reported to the Home Office, threatened with deportation if they missed too many tutorials. Unwilling to suffer that fate and to lose her precious scholarship, she had to force herself to get out of bed and shower. And despite feeling empty and drained, like a vessel tipped upside down, she trudged back to university. Like a ghost, she sat at the back of lecture halls, haunted the corridors, dragged her feet from one seminar to the next. There was no way she would allow herself to be deported. She owed it to herself to succeed academically. It was her only way out.

Anita thought of her illiterate forebears, indentured servants whose generations of hard work and sacrifice had created the foundation for an opportunity like this. She had to keep fighting against the current. No one in her family had ever been afforded such prospects.

To kill time between lectures, she sometimes went to the canteen, where she would sit in a corner with a bowl of salty soup, a bread roll wrapped in cling film and a small carton of Ribena served on a cold tray. Eating alone like that, listening to the conversations of her fellow students but not feeling able to join in, made her feel alienated not only from her classmates but also from herself.

In the evenings, too tired to cook for one, she resorted to pouring boiling water over a Pot Noodle or dunking dry toast in her weak tea. She was used to eating alone standing at the kitchen counter, glancing over her lecture notes, lingering in her solitude while her flatmates went out partying. Buoyed by steaming mugs of instant coffee that scalded her tongue, she pulled all-nighters to catch up with the tutorials she had missed, to finish assignments, or to be able to stay awake to avoid letting the darkness of the night creep into her body.

Sometimes, when she caught herself thinking of home, she wondered what it would be like to think of this cold, rainy place as home. To know people, to be waved at, to be invited to parties. To smile at familiar faces, knowing that her life was here, in this country, and not on some tiny, faraway island across the ocean.

Back in her student room, she sometimes dug in the jar filled with sand and shells. Examining the contents once so familiar, scenes of home would float by and haunt her, taking her back to a place she yearned for, where she could breathe in the humidity, taste the salt in the air and hear the whispers of the sea.

A piece of her had stayed behind when she left Mauritius. The shadow of the girl she used to be no longer seemed to exist. There was no room left for her former self to fit in.

After pulling the lid off her treasured jar of sand and sea-shells, she poured its contents into the toilet and flushed them away. She then tossed the jar into the bathroom bin. After all, they were only a bunch of hollow shells and dead corals.

Not too long afterwards, Anita heard that Professor Beaufort had been awarded an OBE for his lifetime achievements. She found it insulting that someone who had abused his position to take advantage of her could receive a royal distinction and a string of accolades.

It had occurred to her to report his behaviour, but who would take an eighteen-year-old seriously? Who was she to speak out against the archetypal authority figure? Male. Middle-aged. Middle-class. Married. More importantly: white. Wasn't she just some 'exotic' girl from a faraway island which most people had trouble locating on a map? And shouldn't she feel grateful for being given the opportunity to study in England? At a prestigious red-brick university, on a great scholarship?

When the professor asked Anita to meet him again after teaching hours, she refused to go anywhere near him alone. The thought of him made her feel sick. As retribution, the grades he gave her quickly deteriorated from A+ to C−, even though she knew full well that she was more than capable of achieving her goal of a first-class honours degree. She knew she had the potential and the willpower to succeed academically.

And when Anita finally did muster enough courage to approach Belinda Orchard, a senior member of staff who reported directly to the professor, she was stunned by her reaction. Anita had not got far into her account when Miss Orchard started shifting uncomfortably in her chair. The other woman interrupted her, prevented her from speaking and belittled her, making her question her sanity. 'That's just the way he is. Ignore him.' Anita would never forget the condescending way she had addressed her. When she went on to mention the racism she had experienced on campus, she was told that it was not racism and that she was being oversensitive. Miss Orchard hailed from a country notorious for its past colonization of Indigenous people, and there she was, giving Anita a lesson on what constituted racism. From a white person's perspective. 'You just have to accept it,' she added, and patted Anita's hand as if she were an obedient dog before leaving the office. And that was the best advice she could give to Anita, who remained slumped in her chair for several minutes afterwards, shivering. It was clear that Miss Orchard, the cowardly little opportunist, would not go against her boss, but she didn't anticipate what would come next.

A couple of days later, Anita was summoned to a meeting with Benjamin Hall, a well-respected member of the law department. 'Miss Ram,' he started off without preamble, 'I have been led to believe that you have made some very serious accusations against a senior colleague of ours. Without as much as a shred of evidence to support your allegations.' He coldly looked at her through his thick black-framed spectacles.

Without giving her a chance to speak, he sternly went on to inform her that he did not want to hear any such malicious comments or gossip from her ever again, because it amounted to harassment on her part.

When Anita looked at him in shock, unable to believe she was being reprimanded for speaking up, Hall painstakingly went on to explain the term 'harassment' to her. How wrong of her to taint the reputation of the distinguished professor. Without any proof. Putting *his* career at stake. 'We do not tolerate any form of harassment in this institution!' he warned her.

Hall's message was loud and clear. She was expected to conform, to be compliant, to keep her head down and be silent. The system did not reward troublemakers, especially if they were in the minority. As a mere guest in their country, she should play by their rules and be immensely grateful for the opportunity.

Anita was incapable of responding. He was the authority, and she should listen to Him.

*

Years later, Anita would read about how dark-skinned women at her university were treated as second-class citizens and left with no control over their thoughts, feelings and bodies; they were infantilized, threatened and routinely dismissed. Their words carried little weight. They were not allowed to take up as much space as their white counterparts.

Alone in the freezing room, the dazzling white light hanging from the naked bulb cut through Anita's soul. She was unable to move until a friendly Turkish caretaker found her hours later, staring into space, brain still foggy with shock. He kindly informed her that it was late, and that he had to close up for the night. With a distinct click he locked the seminar room behind her, along with all that had happened there. Like a shadow, Anita left the building in the darkness that shrouded her.

At first, Anita was surprised Miss Orchard had mentioned her to Benjamin Hall. It later transpired that Miss Orchard had at that time been having an affair with Professor Beaufort, and that her involvement with him had worked wonders for her career: she had received promotion after promotion. It became apparent that Anita was not the first woman to raise such complaints with Miss Orchard, who, to protect herself, had manipulated Hall, her loyal minion. This had led to her patronizing behaviour towards Anita, whom she saw as a threat to this cosy arrangement.

After a week of absence to recover from her traumatic experience and the subsequent depression it triggered, Anita reluctantly sloped back to her lectures. Although she was physically present during class, mentally she was hovering close to the edge of a pit that almost swallowed her. She asked herself what was worse: to say something and end up being reprimanded for harassment, or to repress the trauma.

As she feared retribution, Anita thought it might be easier to erase that episode altogether, to blank it out like a bad dream. But even bad dreams had a habit of re-emerging every now and then, catching her off guard and harassing her in her sleep.

It turned out that many people in the university knew what was happening. As long as distinguished professor Anthony Beaufort was able to use his stellar academic reputation to secure large grants and funding for the university, they were willing to ignore his behaviour. After all, the university's motto was *in nomine veritatis et honoris*, 'in the name of truth and dignity'. But whose truth? And whose dignity?

A few years later, Anita received an unexpected email. The message, from a friend and colleague at her law firm who had attended the same university, urged her to read the attachment. When Anita clicked on the file, a huge picture of Professor Anthony Beaufort appeared on her screen. It was an article from a broadsheet newspaper stating that two (white) female students had filed a complaint against him for 'extremely inappropriate behaviour'. It was shortly after a new (female) dean had been appointed, one who had finally had the courage to take such allegations seriously. The new dean had immediately suspended the professor – on full pay, of course – as an inquiry was instigated.

More victims decided to come forward to testify against Beaufort, so it did not come as a surprise when, a few months into the inquiry, the university's complaints committee concluded that the professor was guilty of sexually harassing and assaulting female students. The victims all maintained that they had complained, in one form or another, to senior staff members, but that they had been dismissed or intimidated. In a public interview following the findings of the committee, the dean was quoted as saying: 'Looking back, the university should have paid more attention to the victims and acted much sooner. That these issues were not addressed, nor taken seriously, deeply affects me. I cannot begin to imagine what his victims had to endure over the years.'

A wave of relief washed over Anita. The dean's words acted as a balm. And she started to cry, for the defenceless young girl she once was, for all the women subjected to sexual harassment and worse. For those who had been forced to give in, terrified of speaking out against a powerful white man who threatened to harm their careers.

Even though she had been dissuaded from telling her story all those years ago, she admired the women who had the courage to do so, to reclaim their narrative without it backfiring. And at that point, she believed it would be the last time she would be taken advantage of.

Later that evening, after reading the message for the tenth time, Anita's mind had drifted back to her university days. She recalled Miss Orchard and Benjamin Hall, who had chosen to look the other way, and how they had gone to great lengths to protect Professor Anthony Beaufort, their elitist institution and, most importantly, their jobs, at her expense. As soon as the allegations came to light, it was remarkable how Hall and Orchard were the first at the university to condemn the professor's behaviour and issue press releases and internal memos about anti-harassment policy. Putting all the blame on the professor made them feel better about their own complicit behaviour.

What exactly was the definition of rape? Anita wondered. Like the Dutch, French and English colonizers who had raped Mauritius so many years ago?

Again and again her island and her people had been dominated, oppressed, stripped bare, invaded by colonizers. To survive, what choice did they have but to give in and please their powerful masters? She sometimes wondered if the only way to resist was by not resisting.

The island had been desecrated by patriarchy, just as Anita had been by cousins and uncles who had inserted themselves into her childhood, erasing her innocence. As much as Anita tried to bury these memories in shallow graves, they always threatened to resurface every time a tropical cyclone loomed ahead.

13

The showers seemed never-ending. Anita contemplated the beads of water that slowly trickled down the windowpane. Drops kept falling, like infinitesimal mistakes gathering in a pail, a pond, a lake, an ocean.

The constant patter was reminiscent of her former life in London: long rainy weekends spent indoors wrapped in soft chenille with a steaming pot of Earl Grey tea. She would snuggle up to Paul on the sofa while reading the Sunday papers and listening to Edith Piaf.

Bundled in their waterproof parkas and swaddled in cashmere scarves, they would venture out in the rain to a nearby deli on Church Street to pick up some fresh baguette à l'ancienne and pain au chocolat to savour back home. Cheeks fresh from the winter cold, they'd eat in front of the fireplace, letting the crumbs fall messily on the newspapers scattered about. Afterwards, they would lie naked, bodies intertwined, on the thick shagpile rug, flushed from the heat of the crackling fire.

She remembered their particular fit, her slim leg slipping between his pale athletic ones as if their limbs had been fashioned for this purpose only. Paul's body, glowing in the aftermath of lovemaking, had felt strong and safe against her own; she liked to inhale the masculine scent of his skin, his warmth, his hair. With her head on his chest, she allowed herself to feel feminine and protected, her splayed hand resting on his heart. And when she buried her face in his neck, she would often inhale her perfume on his skin. They were happy. At least, she thought they were.

Anita had noticed Paul during her first semester at university, at the Freshers' Fair in the Student Union building. She had felt overwhelmed among the stream of excited first-year students. Back then, she had been an impressionable undergrad law student. He was a slightly older, good-looking economics postgrad. Had history cruelly repeated itself with Nisha?

Receiving the scholarship to study in England was one thing, but how to survive once she got there was another. Answering mock exam questions, solving equations, critical analysis and learning by rote were all skills she had been taught and excelled at. But no one had taught Anita how to navigate unfamiliar waters.

Paul had seemed like a safe haven in the midst of a turbulent, shark-infested sea. University was not at all what Anita had expected. She had imagined professors rushing around clutching dusty books, clad in old-fashioned robes, campuses bedecked with crumbling gargoyles and immaculate English gardens. Instead of ancient college rooms with creaking floors and walls panelled with portraits of fusty scholars glaring down at her, the halls of residence were more modern than she had hoped for. Through the film of jet lag and dépaysement, Anita had found the move across the ocean not only disconcerting but also exhausting.

The first time she saw Paul, she didn't dare take her eyes off him for fear the mirage might disappear. Afterwards, he told her that the first time he saw her velvety eyes he wanted to drown in them: 'There was something in the way you looked at me. I felt a connection, and when you finally turned your gaze, it was like a wave washing over me.' Perhaps Paul had been drawn towards her fragility and humility back then – she was like an injured bird, lost and vulnerable in an unfamiliar environment.

Anita used to see him in the library, where she would spend most of her free time between lectures. Her favourite place was a snug little alcove at the back of the building with large windows overlooking the courtyard. It was right next to the heater, where she could keep warm and hide behind piles of old books, their odour familiar and comforting.

One cold evening shortly after the beginning of the Christmas break, when most students had gone home and Anita felt particularly lonely, she bumped into Paul as the library was about to close. He offered to walk her back to halls. It was a pleasant walk, and he was easy to talk to. So when he casually asked if she'd like to have a quick bite on the way, she found herself accepting his invitation. Anita rarely went out; she could not afford to. Besides, she found it hard to trust people after the incident. She was flattered when he took her to a little Italian place, a couple of streets away from the library.

As soon as they walked in, the waiter recognized him and smiled. They were led to a cosy table for two in front of a kitschy painting of the Colosseum.

'Their pasta's pretty good,' Paul said after the waiter handed them the menus. Without even glancing at it, he ordered a big bowl of home-made gnocchi with sage butter and a bottle of house wine. When their food arrived, she watched him eye the dish approvingly before eating quickly, heartily, sopping up the leftover sauce with chunks of bread. In the candlelit room, she noticed the constant play of light and shadow on his face. Dark blonde strands of hair delicately brushed the contours of his temples, giving him a boyish charm.

After their meal, he asked if she'd like to share a tiramisu.

'I don't think I've had it before. I'm too full, anyway,' Anita said. She wasn't used to alcohol or big meals.

'You've never had tiramisu?' Paul smiled. 'Then all the more reason for you to try it.'

'Sì, sì, signore. A good choice,' the young waiter said, with a sly glance at Anita. She felt herself blush.

After some complimentary limoncello, they finally walked out of the restaurant, only to find out that it had started snowing, tiny, light flakes that fell like delicate petals.

Anita stopped walking, delighted at the scene before her. She had never seen snow before. Giggling like a schoolgirl, she held her head back and offered her face to the snow-white flakes, letting her hair and her thick eyelashes catch the fluffy pieces. She opened her mouth and welcomed the snow on her tongue, a cold, soft sensation, before it quickly melted away. Despite the cold, she felt warm inside.

When Paul reached out his arm to help her tread on the slush, she did not resist. His firm grip felt strangely reassuring as his hand naturally slipped into her soft palm. They walked back hand in hand while the city slowly turned white with powdery icing sugar, like the pretty postcards she had admired as a child. Seeing snow for the first time with Paul felt like one of the most transcendent moments of her life. By the time daffodils started to spring from the campus lawn, their relationship had already blossomed.

Paul's zest for life had fascinated Anita. It was beyond her imagination that someone so eloquent, with a confidence that bordered on arrogance but didn't quite cross the line, would take an interest in her. She had been impressed by his public-school education and the way he enunciated the Queen's

English: something she'd tease him about whenever he made fun of her accent or corrected her pronunciation.

Not only was she eager to assimilate and to emulate, but she was also anxious to please, for nothing meant more to her than his approval. In him, she saw the promise of acceptance: a chance to conceal some aspects of her past, things she considered too shameful to even think about. Anita desperately wanted a normal life, and eventually a family of her own. A new start. A clean slate. And for that she would have done almost anything. Paul seemed earnest about her, and she was happy to reciprocate.

Being Paul's girlfriend, and later his fiancée, elevated Anita's social position to another echelon of society, giving her new leverage, establishing her as someone of intelligence and worth, all things for which she was grateful. He introduced her to his posh friends, who listened to her attentively as if they were at a satsang. To them, she appeared exotic and her words profound. Her silences were no longer deemed socially awkward but deeply contemplative.

In her heart, she was aware these were the very same people who would have otherwise ignored her had she not been with Paul, who liked to parade her on his arm. With him she was invited to up-and-coming artists' vernissages, attended loft parties, visited the theatre, hosted dinners, travelled to places she had read about in books. It was only later, just before their engagement, that she found out about his lineage. Some members of his family had had holdings in the Caribbean, something he shamefacedly told her about after a particularly heavy drinking session. The preferred, curated narrative, however, was that his ancestors had been missionaries who had left Great Britain to convert and educate the Indigenous people.

Despite being only four years older, Paul sometimes had a way of making her feel even younger. When Anita was attending her legal practice course, a tough ordeal before training as a solicitor, her English flatmates failed to understand why she was shopping and cooking for her boyfriend. She bumped into one of them as she came back home with a bagful of fresh laundry.

'Nice Manchester United T-shirt. I didn't realize you were a fan!' her flatmate exclaimed, noticing it on top of the pile of neatly folded clothes.

'Oh. These aren't mine, they're Paul's.'

'And he can't do his washing himself?'

'He's just so busy with his PhD work,' she replied, oblivious to her flatmate's disapproving expression.

So many times, Anita asked herself the same questions. Had she not been a good enough wife? Had she spent too much time at the law firm? Should she have paid him more attention? She mentally tortured herself, wondering if the last couple of years of her marriage had been a sham. The thought of Paul and another, fresher version of herself left a bitter taste in her mouth.

Until a few weeks ago, Anita had believed meeting Paul was the greatest thing ever to have happened to her: he was the first person she had been able to trust again. She had badly wanted to erase her first experience with a white man and give Paul a chance as she basked in his attention. He was her first proper English friend and to some extent had saved her from herself when she thought she was losing her moorings. Unknowingly, he had helped her swim up from the bottom of the ocean. He had grasped her hands and managed to pull her back to the surface.

In retrospect, perhaps she had also found Paul attractive because he was a bit older, an ersatz father to replace the one missing for most of her life. But regardless of how much he had given her, did that justify his actions?

One weekend, shortly after her niece's arrival in London, Anita suggested a spontaneous drive into the countryside and was pleasantly surprised by Paul's enthusiasm at the idea.

'Splendid! Why don't we turn it into a weekend trip? In fact, Mum and Dad are still enjoying a late summer in the south of France. We could use their house for a couple of nights. I'm sure they won't mind.'

'That would be lovely!'

'Next weekend? I could try and finish work at a decent time for once on Friday. And the following morning we could drive to Cambridge early and avoid the traffic. It's not far from their place.'

'And you can take us punting along the Cam, just like in your undergrad days!' Anita chipped in. Paul's excitement was contagious.

'I'd be happy to oblige.'

'Wow, you went to Cambridge? How clever of you!' Nisha looked at him in awe while Paul feigned modesty.

'But only for my undergrad studies,' he added with a boyish smile. 'Then I moved to London for my postgrad.' It amused Anita to see the starstruck look on her niece's face.

Nisha seemed equally eager to leave the city behind and discover the rolling hills of the English countryside. At the time, Anita thought it was charming how her niece wanted to embrace everything Great Britain had to offer.

The previous weekend, Paul had been happy to devote his time to the two women, who from appearances could have been sisters. Enjoying his role as guide, he had pointed out famous landmarks and told funny anecdotes as Nisha drank in every word.

In a matter of days, Nisha had started to imitate his clipped tones and to add a slice of lemon to her tea in lieu of the customary milk and sugar they were used to back on the island. Instead of the Bois Chéri special blend Anita had bought from the Mauritian shop especially for her niece, Nisha developed a penchant for English breakfast and Earl Grey.

Watching Nisha nonchalantly toss her used teabags into the bin, Anita was reminded of when she had been a student on a tight budget, resorting to using each supermarket-brand teabag twice, squeezing out every drop in an attempt to make them last longer. Instead of buying bin liners, she would reuse old plastic bags. Within weeks of her arrival in England, she had mastered the art of shopping cheaply: with loyalty cards, always in the evening (but never on an empty stomach), when most supermarkets drastically reduce prices on short-dated and damaged goods. She discovered that no-frills labels were just as good as fancy packaged items but without the hefty price tags. The best bargains were the slightly damaged or nearly perished food which she had to consume quickly before their expiry date.

The last time Anita had decided to take her niece out to a restaurant, Nisha promptly suggested Japanese. Once in the restaurant, she ordered sushi, sashimi, tataki, edamame and sake without so much as a glance at the prices, with the ease and decadence of the nouveau riche. At the time, Anita thought the girl was struck by the novelty of being away from home and simply indulged her. Perhaps it was her fault for having spoiled her niece, who was starting to take things for granted. But did that explain her niece's attitude towards her? Or were the two women unconsciously playing out Anita's complex relationship with Nisha's mother?

Her niece's behaviour was such a contrast to her own. During her first few days in England, Anita had walked everywhere, feeling small and intimidated in the cold rain that never seemed to stop. She tasted her first scone with clotted cream, and learned how to make egg mayonnaise sandwiches for lunch and to carry her own flask of tea wherever she went.

Discovering the Oxfam shop near the university, crammed with all sorts of second-hand books, had been a revelation and a true source of comfort. At least once a week, she would visit the musty shop to buy books she would quickly devour. One day, she entered the shop cold and shivering.

'Good morning, have you received any new books, preferably in French?' Anita asked.

One look at her soaked jeans and cardigan and the friendly shop assistant took pity on her. She pointed towards the bookshelves, adding, 'But books won't keep you warm, dear. You'll soon be needing a winter coat. Our English winters can be quite unforgiving.'

Unable to afford a new coat, Anita timidly asked the woman if she had any available.

'We just had one donated, in fact. It's as good as new and you're so petite, it should fit you perfectly.' The woman led Anita to the back of the shop, where they were starting to display winter clothes. 'Try it on. The light camel colour will look lovely with your complexion.'

At first, Anita was unsure about the style. But when she removed her shabby, soggy coat to try on the elegant one, she immediately warmed to the way the soft padding cocooned her. She loved the high collar designed to keep out the chill, as well as the elegant belted waist which kept out the draughts. By the time she slipped her hands into the silk-lined pockets, she was in love with the ankle-length coat.

'There, I knew it would fit you like a glove!' The woman took a step back to admire her and seemed genuinely pleased.

Anita looked at the tag. Although it didn't cost much, it was nevertheless more than she could afford.

Sensing her discomfort, the motherly shop assistant assured her that it was genuine cashmere. 'It's a good investment, dear. Once you wear cashmere, you will never want to wear anything else. It's a classic that won't go out of fashion, and the neutral colour will go with everything.'

Anita knew the woman was right. She realized she needed more than a coat, and went to look through a nearby basket. In it, she came across a lovely pair of barely used leather gloves and a bright wool scarf that felt like a caress on her skin, and brought them over to the assistant. She hopefully emptied her drawstring purse onto the counter. After meticulously adding up all her pound coins and smoothing flat her crumpled ten-pound note, she soon realized she didn't have enough. She put away the gloves and the scarf and paid for the coat, which the woman carefully wrapped before handing it to her in a giant carrier bag.

'It was made for you, love. Enjoy!'

Bag in hand, Anita left the shop feeling taller than she had in days. And when she got back to halls, she discovered that the kind woman had surreptitiously slipped the scarf and leather gloves into the bag. That small act of generosity deeply touched her.

She pulled the vintage coat around herself; its warmth was like a hug from an old friend. Glowing from inside, she inhaled its scent, which reminded her of dusty old books. With a new-found confidence, she pushed her feet into her trainers, slipped on the new gloves and threw the scarf around her shoulders for another long walk around the English capital. The coat became her silent companion, shielding her against the bitter cold as she visited parks and famous cemeteries and other landmarks she had read about in her books. Its deep pockets held her note-books and dreams of a future beyond university.

When Paul finally parked in front of his parents' property that Friday evening after work, Anita could sense Nisha's bewilderment as she set eyes on the place for the first time. This bewilderment turned to wonder when they went inside and she took in the understated elegance, elaborate mouldings and numerous corridors.

After a brief tour, they unpacked the few groceries they had picked up on their way out of the city. They had some cheese and wine around the kitchen island and then decided to have an early night. Anita went upstairs with a freshly made cup of tea and a work dossier she still had to finish.

'You go ahead,' Paul told her. 'I'll show Nisha how to switch on the TV and turn on the heater in the guest room. I'll be up in a minute.'

'Goodnight, Nisha. Sweet dreams!'

'Night,' her niece responded, barely looking at her aunt as she followed Paul down the hall towards the second guest room.

The next morning, Anita was surprised to see Paul get up before her and volunteer to make breakfast. 'You're chirpy this morning!' she said.

'It must be all that fresh air,' he shouted from the shower.

As she picked up her work files, she noticed how the untouched tea from the bedside table had now turned cold. A dirty-looking layer of skin had formed on its surface overnight.

A few minutes later, Paul emerged from the steaming-hot bathroom fully dressed. He was wearing his weekend chinos and his favourite navy jumper, which she had once told him brought out the blue in his eyes.

When she went downstairs, Nisha was already in the kitchen leaning against the island with a mug in hand, dressed in newly bought jeans and a sweater, offering her face to the morning light streaming through the French windows. It struck Anita how easy it was for her niece to take everything in, to settle into her new environment, quickly shedding her former skin, looking as if she belonged there. As if she had always been destined for great things.

'Good morning. Sorry I overslept,' Anita said. 'That smells delicious!' Watching her husband playfully flip a pancake in the air, she could not remember the last time he had made her breakfast.

As Anita ate her strawberry jam-filled pancake, she was reminded of an incident during her first visit to the university canteen. In Mauritius, she had been used to a small side portion of chilli with every meal. When she had asked the canteen assistant for some chilli sauce to go with her vegetable pie, the woman explained to her that they did not serve chilli. When Anita took her tray to the cashier, she heard the woman complain to her colleague about 'those bloody pancakes served with vindaloo'. It took her a while to figure out that the woman had in fact said 'those bloody Pakis asking us to serve them vindaloo'. She hoped with all her heart that her niece would not have to endure such insults.

After breakfast, Paul and Anita took Nisha outside to see the garden, since it had been too dark to see anything when they had arrived the evening before. As usual, the lawn was immaculate, laid with the best English turf.

'Paul's parents hosted our wedding right here on this lawn,' Anita said proudly. (What she omitted was how it had only been permitted once they had come around to the idea of their son getting married to a 'girl from the colonies').

'Gosh, everything is so beautiful here!' Nisha exclaimed as she wandered about the lawn overlooked by the distant hills.

'Your parents couldn't attend the wedding because you'd broken your leg a few days before,' Anita said.

'I remember! Nani did say how magical it was, but I thought it was a hired venue. I had no idea it belonged to Paul's family!'

Anita sometimes wondered if it was a rebellious streak in him which had prompted Paul to marry her, demonstrating his open-mindedness to the world despite his conventional upper-middle-class upbringing. She remembered how after the wedding he would show her off at work events, encouraging her to wear a sari. He would introduce her to his partners and senior colleagues, showcasing his liberalism to compensate for or to balance out his conservative background.

Strolling around the landscaped garden, they admired the neatly trimmed hedges and the profusion of flowers in what appeared to be a carefully managed display of riotous colours and controlled wilderness. Anita thought of the crops her dada had cultivated with his own hands: sugar cane, mangoes, breadfruit, avocados, lychees, atemoyas, Java apples, starfruit and so much more. He liked to visit family and friends with a bagful of bergamot, a bunch of bananas or a couple of ripe papayas, because for him harvests were meant for sharing.

As a child, Anita had craved a flower or two and had asked her dada whether he could plant some. He told her that flowers were for the rich. There was no room in his plot for the luxury of flowers or ornamental plants. So the first thing she did when they finally bought their house in London was to plant lavender, thyme, sage, rosemary and an elderflower bush. Fragrant, colourful and yet edible, she knew her dada would have approved.

When Anita was about eight, Dada was frustrated that one of the olive trees he had nurtured for years was bearing no fruit. Condemning the tree, he had cursed before barking orders at Serge, his garden helper. '*Bizin koup li sa, pie la napa raporte. Li pa vo nanye!*' Chop down the fruitless tree. It's absolutely useless! For him, a barren tree was a waste of good space in the orchard.

Soon enough, the olive tree was replaced by a mango sapling unearthed from the nursery. The seed seemed to thrive in the fertile soil and eventually turned into a lush tree which delivered smooth, golden mangoes, year after year. It was of the Maison Rouge variety, considered by Mauritians to be by far the tastiest. She remembered how, after squeezing the fruit, she would tear a small strip off its top with her teeth before biting into its flesh. The juice would trickle down her throat and neck, dousing her in a sweet, ripe scent that lingered for hours. And when her dada passed away, his plants continued searching for the sun, even in his absence, and the fruit quietly ripened, nourishing those left behind.

Seeing Paul walk tall and proud towards his parents' country house, Anita was painfully reminded that there was a legacy to uphold and to pass down to his heir. It came with a sense of duty, and an obligation to carry on the family name.

I 5

Anita tied her hair back in a messy ponytail and put on a baggy pair of cut-offs and a faded T-shirt before spreading several layers of old newspaper on the floor, making sure no area was left uncovered. Using different lengths of tape, she methodically masked along the wooden skirting boards, the window and door frames and escutcheons. She covered the few pieces of furniture with frayed cotton sheets that were dotted with mildew.

She held on to the can of paint with one hand and used the other to stir it with a wooden stick. Then she inhaled the pungent odour before dipping her brand-new roller into the thick emulsion. It was satisfying to listen to the swish of the roller as it moved up and down the bedroom wall, wiping out its former grubbiness and replacing it with a glossy layer of fresh olive green.

Beads of sweat began to drip down her face after she had been painting for an hour. Her T-shirt clung to her body, and there were damp, clammy patches beneath her arms. Her feet were bare, her arms and legs flecked with paint. Feeling slightly overwhelmed by the labour, Anita wiped her face with the back of her hand and decided to take a break.

While rinsing the brushes in the outside sink, memories of her former life with Paul, the long weekends spent renovating their Victorian terraced house in London, flashed back intermittently. She vividly remembered those first few days in their new home: relishing the space and emptiness of the well-lit rooms waiting to be filled, walking around the house barefoot, feeling the warmth of the creaky wooden boards underneath her feet. She and Paul made plans: which herbs to plant in their small patch of green, which wedding pictures to hang on the empty walls, and how to choose the perfect pastel colour for the nursery. She loved the thrill and excitement of visualizing and decorating each room, painting samples on the walls, visiting antique shops and flea markets hunting for bargains.

Once, they stumbled across an ancient stone hearth in a vintage shop in Hackney, which they thoroughly cleaned and installed in the living room as a *pièce de résistance*, next to a neat pile of logs. They had spent a ridiculous amount of money on a pristine white kitchen that showed off the gleaming solid oak parquet which they had lovingly sanded and polished. The walls were hung with framed vintage prints of aromatic herbs and plants. An arrangement of Delftware, dozens of cookery books and several copper skillets was neatly displayed on open shelves.

She loved how the newly waxed living room floorboards shone in the light of a roaring fire, and the way the large antique mirror over the mantelpiece reflected the scented candles on the deep-silled window. But she was most proud of the built-in bookcase they had installed on the wall, which she affection-ately referred to as 'the library'. The floor-to-ceiling shelves were crammed with novels, travel guides, essays, monographs of various artists, old atlases, biographies, coffee table books and even a few children's classics Anita had surreptitiously bought in the hope that she would one day be able to read them to their children. Many happy hours were spent in that room, curled up with a favourite book while the sun filtered through the windows, which were deliberately left unadorned to empha-size the room's generous proportions.

Tears temporarily blurred her vision. Eager to brush away the memories, Anita washed the stains off her hands under the cold running water. She scrubbed them vigorously with a bar of soap and a pumice stone until no flecks were left on her skin and her hands had become red and sore. Using a stiff towel, she patted her hands dry before venturing into the kitchen, where Ma was busy preparing lunch. 'Do you need some help?' she asked.

'You could clean the rice.' Ma tilted her head towards the ten-kilo jute bag of rice stored in a corner of the kitchen.

Anita scooped out one large cup of rice from the bag before soaking it in a deksi filled with lukewarm water. With the help of a plastic spatula, she carefully fished out the debris floating on the surface of the cloudy water. She rinsed off the rice and handed the pot to her mother, who placed it on the stove to cook.

Ma had boiled some water earlier and left it to cool in a plastic jug on the kitchen counter. Anita poured herself a large glass and added some ice cubes. Sipping her drink, she watched her mother spread old sheets of newspaper on the floor before sitting cross-legged on them.

First, Ma used plain flour, warm water and oil to prepare the dough for rotis. She kneaded the mixture firmly, her fists in rhythm with the ticking grandfather clock. Once it reached the ideal texture, soft without being sticky, she covered the dough with a fresh tea towel and set it aside to rest, so that they would be light and fluffy.

Using a sharp knife, its blade more black than silver, Ma then scraped, peeled and hacked vegetables without ever having recourse to a chopping board, a skill Anita could not master without risking serious injury. She swiftly crushed garlic cloves with the side of the blade. Breaking a lumpy finger of ginger into half, she grated its skin off within seconds and dropped it into the stone mortar before adding a chunk of fresh turmeric. With the help of a thick stone pestle, she pounded and ground until the mixture reached a smooth, aromatic paste. Next, she split a whole carrot into quarters before slicing them into thin matchsticks, which she tossed with mustard seeds, oil and fresh green chillies from the garden to make zasar, spicy pickle.

Ma looked content as she efficiently hacked beetroot, chay-otes, cabbages, okra and cauliflowers into rings, dices, florets, shreds and slices. She was surrounded by an assortment of ceramic bowls, plastic receptacles and colanders, in which she neatly stowed the chopped, colourful vegetables into piles.

This was one of Ma's qualities: her ability to lead a simple, frugal life with the help of her late husband's small pension. She had a no-nonsense air about her, making the best of what she had and meticulously putting aside the maximum pos-sible, like her ancestors before her. She was also the owner of a small plot of land inherited from her father's side, including tea plantations near the Bois Chéri estate, which her broth-ers cultivated on her behalf. During school holidays, Anita used to help Nani, her maternal grandmother, pick baskets of tea leaves which were then sold by weight to the nearby fac-tory. Nani didn't want her granddaughter to work the fields and end up as a labourer like practically all the women before her, but Anita insisted on helping out. And so she woke up at dawn and waded, still drowsy with sleep, into the sea of green with the rest of the seasonal workers who greeted each other in Bhojpuri. She dutifully picked the first three leaves of each tea shrub, as Nani had taught her. Making sure they were perfect and uncrushed, she would select the most delicate new shoots. From a young age, she became aware of how many hours of labour went into producing one pot of sweet, milky tea. And as she grew older, this awareness led Anita to develop a complicated relationship with sugar and tea, the two crops that her family had grown out of.

Anita's maternal and paternal families could trace their origins a long way back, so deeply rooted and ingrained were they into the island's rich history. And it was not without a sense of wonder that Anita thought of her forebears who had travelled from Bihar to Mauritius aboard the *Malda* with nothing but their dreams. They had managed to acquire property from their masters, who exploited the caste system to assign plantation roles and land. Anita's great-grandparents, who were mere coolies from India, had become landowners despite being illiterate. After the abolition of slavery, they had been part of the wave of migration known as the Great Experiment, whereby the British used Mauritius to test the system of coercing labourers to come to the island and work on its thriving plantations. Its success led to other former colonial powers using the same method for their dependencies around the world – which was just a(nother) sanitized form of slavery.

Ma was a creature of routine, and even after the death of her husband and despite living alone, she still cooked almost every day. It was hard for her to imagine a life that did not revolve around food. The importance of dinner rituals in her family was another legacy passed down by her Indian ancestors, whose meals back then were mostly vegetarian. As unlettered indentured labourers, it was a way of keeping alive their memories and traditions from Mother India. Generations later, they still cooked on open fires using the most rudimentary utensils.

By the light of a flickering flame, they would eat toufe sousou, satini pipangay and zasar bilinbi from banana leaves with freshly made dal puri cooked on a flat tawa over charcoal.

As much as Anita loved and respected her mother, she had silently prayed that she would never end up alone like her. It was not a life she aspired to. Her very first memories were of playing under the kitchen table as Ma concocted one dish after another, breathing in the hot smells that emanated from the stove: creamy gros pois bubbling in a big karay, perfectly puffed-up rotis, freshly chopped coriander from the garden. Even when Ma had visited Anita in London, she had insisted on cooking every day, much to Paul's ill-disguised revulsion at the strong smells that invaded their immaculate kitchen. Her dishes did not seem to sit well with his delicate English stomach. It pained her now to think how she had shed so much of her own culture in her efforts to assimilate, and to acquire his.

After dribbling some oil into the hot karay, Anita helped Ma fry a handful of okra in a crackle of garlic and mustard seeds. Once the feast was ready and the air was infused with the smell of curry, they sat down at the plastic table and ate in silence, for Ma was never chatty at mealtimes.

The old Indian songs from the radio occasionally broke the silence. Anita tore off a piece of hot roti and let the mild buttery flavour settle on her tongue. Like Ma, she used her fingers to eat, first making a small ball of rice and then mixing it with different vegetable dishes. She enjoyed the way the spicy pickles made the back of her mouth tingle.

Back in London, Anita had avoided making curries because of Paul's intolerance to garlic and spices. Even though she loved seafood, he had an allergy to shellfish. Eating with her fingers was something she never did in London for fear of offending her partner, who was perhaps not as comfortable with certain aspects of her culture as he ought to have been, and as he pretended to be.

After washing the dishes in the sink, Anita borrowed the radio from the kitchen and plugged it into a corner of her room. She carried on painting the walls listening to pop music occasionally interrupted by the cheerful voice of the disc jockey. She did not hear the phone ring, nor Ma entering the room with a slightly puzzled look on her face. 'It's for you,' she said, holding up the phone, pulling the cord as far as it would go.

'Who is it?' Anita assumed it was one of her nosy relatives and hoped it was not her sister, with whom she had no inclination to speak. Perched on the wooden ladder, she was about to tell Ma that she was once again indisposed, when something in her mother's expression stopped her.

'It's someone called Siven?'

'Siven? Are you sure? I don't know anyone called Siven.'

'He has an accent,' Ma said, shrugging.

Intrigued, Anita stepped down the ladder and placed the dripping brush back on the tray. A thought struck her. 'Do you mean Sven?' she asked, brow creased.

'Yes. It's a man.'

Anita quickly wiped her smeared hands on a rag before taking the phone from her mother. 'Hello?' she said softly into the receiver.

'Hallo Anita. It's Sven,' he said, sounding slightly nervous. He continued speaking rapidly, without pausing. 'I hope you don't mind me calling. I looked you up in the phone directory. There are not many Rams living in Palma. How are you?'

'I'm good, thanks. Is Maya okay?' Anita asked cautiously.

'Ja, she's okay. In fact, that's why I'm calling. She said you had not been to the beach the last three days, so we got a bit concerned and wondered if you were ill or something.'

Anita felt slightly guilty as she remembered that the last time she had met Maya on the beach, she had casually said she would see her again the next day. The child had obviously taken her words for granted. 'Thanks. I'm fine,' she answered, aware that Ma was hovering nearby, seemingly engrossed in cleaning the corridor near her room.

'We're glad to hear that. Aren't we, Maya?'

Anita could not help but smile to herself as she heard his daughter's babble in the background. 'I've been busy sorting out a few things at home,' she said, fiddling with the phone extension.

'And we thought you had decided to go back to the land of Her gracious Majesty.'

'Back to London? No way!' Her reply came out sharper than she had intended, causing Ma to look up from her task. Did she sense relief at the other end, or was it her imagination?

'We were wondering if perhaps you would like to join us for Kaffee und Kuchen – sorry, I mean coffee and cake – on Friday afternoon?'

Anita hesitated for a few seconds. 'This Friday?' she asked.

'Ja. I usually finish work early on Fridays.'

'That's tomorrow.'

'If you have time, that is.'

Pondering how to respond to the unexpected invitation, Anita twisted and untwisted the phone line between her sticky fingers.

'Maya would love to see you,' Sven added, almost as an afterthought.

'Sure. Why not?' It wasn't as if Anita had better things to do.

'When you drive towards Tamarin, our house is on the coastal road –'

'I don't have a car,' Anita interrupted, immediately regretting her defensive tone.

'It's within walking distance of the bus stop,' Sven said.

Anita carefully jotted down the directions to their property. By the time she had placed the brownish receiver down, she felt slightly light-headed. There were green traces on its dull surface from her fingertips. As she turned around, she saw Ma staring at her, unable to hide her disapproval. 'Who was that man?' she asked, pursing her lips.

'Someone I met on the beach.' Anita realized how blasé her reply sounded to Ma.

'A foreigner?'

'He has a daughter,' Anita added by way of explanation. She picked up her brush and hastily dunked it into the can. Her sudden movement sent around a spray of olive green, which splashed messily on her arms and clothes. She began trying to wipe the stains from her denim shorts.

'Why did he call you?' Ma demanded.

'I befriended his little girl on the beach, and now she wants to see me.'

Ma looked unconvinced. 'A married man! What about the child's mother?'

'I don't think they live together,' Anita said. By now she had given up trying to remove the paint from her shorts.

'Is this a good idea? Look what happened the last time you got involved with a blan! Your grandfather was right. Remember how they treated him on their estates? They've been exploiting us for centuries. The number of light-skinned children those patrons bequeathed to tea-pickers whenever they fancied! It's in their blood. The whites are not to be trusted!' warned Ma, storming out of the room before Anita could answer.

Suppressing her mounting irritation, Anita carried on painting, listening to the upbeat songs blaring from the radio. Peering out of the window, she noticed that the earlier rain had been replaced by the sun, which had made an appearance from behind the clouds. The colour of the fresh coat on the wall, which had seemed overpowering at the beginning, had started to dry and reveal a soothing shade that reminded her of the olive groves she had visited with Paul during a Tuscan escape one late summer.

16

The next morning, Anita breathed in the cloying smell of paint and surveyed the once-familiar bedroom. As she took in the transformation, she realized that, day after day, she was making slow but steady progress. Traces of the previous grubby colour had been wiped away.

She had relocated the bed next to the window. Having discarded the broken wardrobe, she used Ma's vintage trunk to store her few pieces of clothing. She had repainted the bed frame, desk and wooden shelf a slightly distressed off-white colour. After sanding an old wooden crate, she had applied a layer of varnish before turning it into a bedside table. She decorated it with freshly cut frangipanis from Ma's garden, which she placed in an Orangina bottle next to her books and the cowrie shells she had collected with Maya. The sweet fragrance of the flowers mingled pleasantly with the smell of fresh paint.

The empty space in the corner had been filled with a luscious plant in a ceramic pot bought at the DIY store in Tamarin. Its crisp large leaves with their light-green patterns added some life to the room. The faded, childish curtains had been torn down and replaced by a plain off-white calico set that billowed gently in the breeze.

Anita looked at the austere room, stripped and bleached to her satisfaction, and was filled with peace. This was her life, at least for now, until she could work things out and clear her head. Decluttered and emptied of its former jumble, the room was now looking more spacious than before.

'Look at all the empty space you have left. How are we going to fill it?' Ma asked.

'I need lots of space to be able to think clearly,' Anita murmured.

Ma looked as if she was about to say something, but then sighed and shook her head instead.

That night, Anita was overcome by a strange sense of achievement as she climbed into bed with a cup of vanilla tea and her beloved copy of Jean-Marie Gustave Le Clézio's *L'Africain*. She understood the wisdom in a quiet cup of sweet Mauritian tea. English tea was so overrated.

I 7

Anita consulted the address she had jotted down on a piece of paper. The instructions were clear: she had to walk past the Tamarin salt pans along the coastal road and turn right into a small residential lane opposite the boat repair shop. Sven had told her on the phone to look for the third house after the sea almond tree, the one with a slanted roof.

She got off the bus one stop early and decided to meander along past the deserted Tamarin salt pans. A couple of carefree goats were busy munching on the weeds bordering the main road. It was surprising how the traditional method of producing salt, started by French settlers in the eighteenth century, had stood the test of time. A quiet, laid-back atmosphere reigned over the area, which was dominated by pans made of volcanic stones that were assembled into a network of canals into which seawater was pumped. The water in the shallow squares of rock would slowly evaporate, leaving a thin, delicate crust on its surface known as fleur de sel. Fleur de sel was known for its complex mineral flavours and crunchy texture. Some referred to it as 'the caviar of salt'.

Anita reached the private alley off the coastal road and was taken aback by the multitude of flowers that bordered the path. She stroked a cluster of frangipani blossoms, letting her fingers linger on their small wax-like petals. As she lifted her face to inhale the scent, standing on her toes as poised as a ballet dancer, a car drove past her.

A set of automatic gates slid open as the vehicle turned into a driveway lined with indigenous bottle palm trees. The

PRIYA HEIN

beachfront property, nestled in a lush tropical garden, was slightly intimidating.

After parking next to a neatly trimmed bougainvillea hedge, Sven got out of the car. It was the first time she had seen him wear a tie, and it gave him a slight air of authority. His linen suit smelled fresh despite the heat.

'Hallo Anita.'

'Hi!'

'I see you like frangipanis?' He removed his sunglasses and his metallic blue eyes seemed to look right through her.

Anita hadn't realized she was still holding a single frangipani. Her cheeks burned with embarrassment at being caught red-handed. 'They're my favourite flowers,' she said. 'There's something about their scent that reminds me of my childhood. But I didn't pick it. It was already on the ground,' she added a little defensively.

'I'm only teasing you! And besides, I'm pretty sure Alain, our gardener, won't mind. Aren't they supposed to represent new beginnings?' He smiled.

'Yes, Hindus use garlands of frangipanis during weddings to symbolize the couple's new life together.' Anita's face clouded slightly as she recalled her own wedding.

'They are rather exquisite, aren't they?'

In response, Anita lifted the flower to her face and breathed in its perfume.

'I hope you didn't have too much trouble finding the house?' Sven asked, pulling his leather briefcase out of the car.

'Not at all. Thanks for the clear directions.'

'This way,' he said.

Anita followed Sven as he ushered her through the back door into the open-plan kitchen. He threw the car keys on the vide poche and dropped his briefcase on the counter before switching on the ventilator. The throttle of the ceiling fan whisking into life echoed slightly in the high-ceilinged house.

'Even after years of living on the island, I'm still not used to the tropical heat.' He shrugged apologetically before loosening his tie and rolling up his sleeves. Anita could see tiny beads of perspiration on his temples. 'Can I get you something to drink?'

Anita hesitated. 'Just some water, please.'

Sven took out two glasses from the range of fitted cupboards above the sink and poured cold water into one, before making himself a large gin and tonic from the bar. As he removed ice cubes from the fridge, she noticed that his arms were covered in hairs similar to the golden-brown fibres that peeled off the fresh coconut husks her dada used to plant.

'So how was your day?' Anita said, feeling the need to talk to hide her nervousness.

'Tedious. I spent hours with clients inspecting construction sites on the east coast. I hope yours was better than mine!' Sven dropped the ice into his glass.

Not wanting to talk about her quiet day shadowing Ma as she carried out various household chores, Anita took a sip of water and asked after Maya instead.

'She'll be very pleased to see you. The little monkey's probably on the beach with her nanny. Perhaps we should join them.' He picked up his glass. 'It's this way.'

Anita followed him into the living room, which was sparsely furnished with a large rattan sofa and a glass coffee table stacked with glossy German architectural magazines. 'Fantastic house!' she enthused.

'Thanks. It's just that since Vanessa – Maya's mother – left, the house has been quite empty. We never got round to finishing it.' He almost tripped over a soft African doll lying on the sand-coloured tiles. He picked it up and dropped it in a nearby wooden trunk full of Maya's toys and picture books.

Anita's attention was caught by a colourful nude, prominently displayed in the centre of the otherwise bare wall. 'Is that an original Vaco Baissac?'

'Yes, it is. We got it a couple of years ago. Vanessa was drawn to that particular piece, so we bought it on a whim.'

With its vibrant colours, the painting captured the simple landscape of the Mauritian countryside and featured a Creole woman, with soft curves and ample hips, as its focal point. Anita was conscious of Sven's gaze on her as her own eyes zigzagged over the large canvas, taking in all the details of her shapely silhouette.

'*Une belle dame créole,*' Sven murmured.

'*Au pays parfumé que le soleil caresse, la brune enchanteresse,*' Anita replied automatically, reciting the rest of Baudelaire's poem.

'Indeed! Do you like it?'

Anita nodded and talked about the play of colours in the light and the distinct forms of figure and objects in the painting. 'I like Vaco Baissac's vibrant paintings, but I prefer the work of his brother, Jean-Claude Baissac, and his original themes.'

'Me too!' Sven's face became more animated at the mention of the lesser-known artist's name. 'I'm also a fan of his brother, but Vanessa prefers Vaco, who's more famous and very popular with tourists.'

'Are you familiar with the bold oil paintings of the young Mauritian artist Dany Lebrun?'

'No, I'm afraid I'm not,' he said sheepishly.

'His fluid contours, made with unfettered brushstrokes, remind me of the nudes of Henri Matisse during his brief Fauvist phase.'

'You seem to know a lot about art.'

'Not really. I'm just bluffing.' Anita turned to face him, smiling.

'Well in that case, you bluff really well.'

Anita's gaze went back to the nude as she took another sip of water. The notion of the white male's fetishism of an 'exotic' body floated at the back of her mind. The colourful painting looked out of place in the house, dominating the dining area where Sven presumably sat at dinner time. It was odd to think that he would be positioned underneath the full-sized image every time he sat down to eat. She wondered if the artwork was a malicious remnant of his ex-wife. A constant mockery.

As if he could read her thoughts, Sven half-jokingly told her that the painting was a reminder of what the house was lacking – a feminine touch, personality and colour. 'When she left, I couldn't be bothered to take it down,' he added more quietly.

'When did she leave?'

Sven hesitated with his glass halfway to his lips. 'Almost two years ago.' His eyes briefly met hers before looking away.

Anita glanced at her feet, unable to find a fitting response. Although his ex-wife was physically not there, and despite Sven's earlier statement, Anita could still sense her everywhere. Her absence was almost a presence in itself.

'Come, let's go find Maya,' Sven said abruptly. 'She's probably impatient to see you.' He downed the rest of his drink and led her outside.

It struck Anita that Sven's disposition had changed. He seemed different from the nonchalant person she had met on the beach a few days ago. Or perhaps her perception of him had changed.

Anita followed Sven across the room and waited for him to open the sliding doors overlooking the sea. She was awed by the view that greeted her as soon as she stepped out onto the terrace. The expanse of the clear blue lagoon, only a few metres from the house, took her breath away. There were no sounds except for the faint lapping of the waves on the sand.

'A view to die for!' Anita was aware that a pieds-dans-l'eau property was a privilege very few could afford. Many owners had to sell or rent out their bungalows when they could no longer keep up with the high taxes imposed on beachfront properties.

'We got this place because of its view. I'll never tire of looking out at the sea. Its colour is never quite the same from one minute to the next. It's an extraordinary palette of shades and nuances.' His gaze went beyond the horizon.

'And now you're the one who sounds like an artist!' Anita teased him.

'Ah! So you think you're the only one who knows how to bluff?' Sven turned around, grinning, to face her.

'Touché!'

The view had a soothing effect as they stood side by side, taking in the splendour of the ocean that melted into the horizon. From the terrace, Anita could see the distant figures of Sven's daughter and her nanny by the low tide pools near the rocks.

After removing his office shoes and peeling off his socks, which he discarded in a corner of the terrace, Sven decided to descend the few steps to open the latch of the wooden gate that separated the house from the beach. Together, he and Anita strolled barefoot on the sand towards Maya, who was engrossed in the task of decorating a sandcastle with shells. The child was blissfully unaware of their presence.

On their way, they passed a young family. The mother and father were each holding one of their little boy's hands, lifting him in the air and swinging his body every few steps before setting him down again on the sand. The boy, who was wearing bright orange shorts, chuckled with delight before shouting 'Ankor! Ankor!'

'Papa! Anita!' Maya's angelic face lit up as soon as she saw them approaching. '*Schau was ich gemacht habe!* Look what I made!' She proudly pointed at her creation.

'*Hallo mein Sonnenschein!*' Sven greeted his little girl with a hug. '*Das hast du toll gemacht!* Well done!' He picked her up and swirled her around, laughing.

As soon as Sven put her down on the sand, Maya rushed into Anita's arms. 'Anita! Endlich! You have come to see me!' she exclaimed in her sing-song voice.

'Hello, Maya. It's lovely to see you. How are you?' Anita was slightly taken aback by the child's display of affection. She ruffled her wavy hair fondly before securing the single frangipani behind her ear with the help of a hair clip she had bought at the bazaar. 'There! Beautiful island girl,' said Anita with satisfaction.

'Where have you been? I thought you left on the big Flugzeug,' Maya asked Anita accusingly.

'*Sag bitte danke fürs Geschenk!* Say thank you for the gift, Maya!' said Sven.

'You did not come to see me on the beach!' Maya carried on, ignoring her father's request.

'No, I'm sorry. I was busy with a project.'

'What's a project?'

'*Das ist wie Arbeit.* It's like work,' said Sven.

'Ah so! My Papa has a lot of Arbeit.'

'I'm sure he does.'

'Maya likes to speak Denglish, a mixture of Deutsch and English,' Sven said with a grin.

'So I've noticed.' Anita winked at the child, who was basking in the attention.

'Anita, come and see my new train set and Barbie-Puppe. My Oma und Opa sent them to me from Deutschland,' Maya said as proud as a peacock.

Anita found the girl's enthusiasm refreshing. 'Oh, I'd love to!'

Maya slipped her small hand into Anita's and together they walked back to the house. The ebbing tide had formed ripples in the sand, and she enjoyed walking on the ridges that gently massaged her soles. On the way they stopped to examine the small pools of water by the rocks. Anita was struck by a bed of shiny cowrie shells begging to be picked; she wished she could reach down into the clear water and stroke the pearly surface that gleamed in the sunlight. As she climbed the stone steps leading up to the terrace with wet, sandy feet, she was aware of Sven only a few centimetres behind her.

When Anita and Maya were alone in the child's bedroom some minutes later, admiring her collection of board books and toys, Anita noticed a picture that immediately piqued her interest. It was a framed family shot featuring a slightly younger-looking Sven with an attractive woman who was holding baby Maya in her arms. The woman's thick black wavy hair, a typical feature of Mauritians of African descent, framed her heart-shaped face. From her earlobes hung big silver hoops. She had on a pale bias-cut summer dress which accentuated her dark, velvety skin. At the end of her long slender legs were jewel-studded mules. Anita stared at the woman's cheekbones and dazzling smile.

Normally Anita felt comfortable with her demure look, but she suddenly felt dowdy. Tugging her plain white peasant top over the waist of her jeans, she felt like she would never be able to dress with as much panache. She was dying to ask Maya about her mother, but she did not dare for fear of spoiling something tender.

At that point Sven popped his head round the door to announce that Kaffee und Kuchen were ready. 'We're just putting Maya's toys away, we'll be down in a sec,' Anita responded.

As she walked past the bathroom, Anita noticed a woman's Chinese-style peignoir hanging from a peg and thought she could detect wisps of a flowery perfume lingering in the air – a reminder that someone had already been there, had marked her territory. Through a door that had been left slightly ajar, she caught a glimpse of a wooden four-poster bed with a muslin canopy. She felt like an intruder and hurriedly followed Maya down the stairs to join her father, who was cajoling her with promises of cake.

Anita joined the others on the terrace. The nanny had already placed a steaming pot of tea on a large wooden table overlooking the sea, and on a silver etagere she arranged an assortment of petits fours including mini tartes aux bananes and napolitaines covered in pink icing.

The seating area was next to an ancient tamarind tree that stood tall and graceful. Its foliage was feathery with a few hanging pods. Anita picked a pod from one of the lower branches and snapped it open. It had a bittersweet, pungent smell.

'Didn't Tamarin get its name from these groves?' Sven asked her as he lifted Maya onto her chair.

'Tamarin was named after the river that flowed into the bay, from that mountain range over there.' Anita pointed towards the valley. 'The river, in turn, was named after the gigantic tamarind trees that thrived along its banks.' She took her seat next to the child. 'According to Hindu beliefs, tamarind trees are inhabited by ghosts and spirits.' She smiled at Maya, who perked up at the mention of ghosts. They admired the view of the bay populated with the tamarind groves that had a slight eldritch feel to them. Trees that had stood tall for centuries, relics of the past.

'I prefer coffee, but please help yourself to some Mauritian tea,' said Sven, changing the subject, before biting into a generous piece of cake.

Anita poured herself a cup of tea and watched Maya gulp down her glass of milk and wipe her mouth on her sleeve. The child proceeded to scoff one napolitaine after another, blissfully unaware of the mess the crumbs were making as they fell on the table. Every now and then she would lick her sugary fingers before wiping them on her dress. There were bits of pink icing and guava jam stuck to the corners of her mouth.

'*Bitte pass auf!* Careful, Maya!' Sven gently reprimanded his daughter.

Filled with longing, Anita watched Maya and wondered what it was that connected her to the child. Instinctively, she took a paper napkin and started wiping the girl's face, then removed the small lumps of icing that had managed to get stuck in her messy curls.

'*Danke schön,*' said Maya as she piled three more napolitaines onto her plastic plate.

'*Das ist genug*. Enough!' her dad gently scolded as Maya pulled a face and started sulking.

From the corner of her eye, Anita was aware the nanny was staring at her oddly. She had the distinct feeling the older woman was questioning Anita's role in the household. She felt like a fraud, and to mask this took a big gulp of the burning-hot liquid and ended up scalding her tongue.

'*Sollen wir schwimmen gehen?*' Sven asked while helping the nanny clear the table.

'Nein!' Maya shook her head.

Ignoring her, Sven turned his attention to Anita. 'I usually go for a swim with Maya after work. Would you like to join us?' he asked.

'I would love to, but I didn't bring my swimsuit.'

'That's a pity. Although I have a feeling this has not stopped you before.' He grinned.

Anita looked away.

'*Nicht heute, Papa*. No swimming today! I just want to play with Anita,' pouted Maya, elbows on the table. It was clear she did not like being left out of the conversation. The way the child was behaving gave the impression that she seldom had visitors to play with.

'*Bist du sicher?* Are you sure?' asked Sven, but the child only shook her head. Slightly placated by the prospect of playing with Anita, she remained adamant about not wanting to swim. The smile of satisfaction on the little girl's face suggested she was used to having her own way. It became apparent that the child wanted Anita's attention all to herself, and clung to her like a barnacle. Had Anita decided to swim, Maya would have probably joined her in order not to miss out.

A few minutes later, Anita and Maya sat down on the shore, making moulds of sand with the girl's toys as Sven waded into the ocean. He dived in confidently, arms stretched out. Anita watched him cut through the lagoon with swift, athletic strokes, his body becoming smaller and smaller as he effortlessly swam towards the reef before turning back. Some minutes later, he emerged from the sea and picked up his towel from the sand. Anita noticed how the small pearls of water on his golden skin reflected the late-afternoon sun, causing his body to shimmer. She quickly averted her gaze when she caught a glimpse of the dark-brown hairs that clung together at the base of his taut stomach.

The sun was lazily making its descent into the lagoon when the three of them headed back to the house. Anita said good-bye to Maya and her nanny once the child was settled and in her pyjamas, smelling deliciously of soap and warm milk.

It was already dark when Sven drove Anita home, hair still damp from his post-swim shower. The street, lined with sugar cane fields, was poorly lit. She sat stiffly in the passenger seat, acutely aware of his proximity. From the corner of her eye, she observed how he manoeuvred the car with ease: steering with one hand, casually resting the other on his thigh, his eyes seldom leaving the road ahead.

Anita directed him to the house, knowing Ma would be waiting for her before having dinner. She could clearly picture her mother fretting and peering through the window every five minutes, killing time as she awaited her daughter's arrival.

'Thank you for your visit. It meant a lot to Maya,' Sven said before turning off the engine in front of the dimly lit house.

'It was a pleasure. Thanks for the invitation. You have such a sweet girl.'

'*Ein kleiner Affe.* A real little monkey,' he added affectionately. 'And as I'm sure you've noticed, she can be very insecure at times. She's scared I'll leave her too,' he added, as if to himself. Anita was unsure how to respond to this.

She was already out of the car when she heard the buzz of the window rolling down. 'Anita?' Sven called out in the semi-darkness.

'Yes?' She turned around, thinking she had left something behind.

'Would you like to have a drink with me? Without Maya? It'd be nice to have an uninterrupted adult conversation for once. This weekend? I could pick you up.' Slightly taken aback by the invitation, Anita struggled to find an answer. He must have sensed her reluctance, for he quickly added: 'Think about it and let me know.' He offered her one of his business cards. Leaning against the door, she hesitantly took the piece of paper from him. Their fingers touched lightly. The sudden intimacy troubled her.

That night, Anita had the same dream about the little girl dancing on a moonlit beach. Again, the same thing happened: each time she reached for the tiny, spectral figure, the girl simply drifted back into the shadows.

1 8

It was a warm, breezy evening. The taxi turned into the drive of the hotel, which was lined with lush tropical plants. When Anita got out of the car, a gentle wind coming from the ocean caressed the branches of a flame tree, causing red petals to fall over her like a blessing. She entered the lobby and trod carefully across the marble floor in her high heels, conscious of her posture.

'Good evening, miss. How may I help you?' said the friendly concierge.

'Hello, I'm meeting a friend. Mr Steinacher?' Anita replied, trying to hide her pleasure at being addressed as *miss* instead of *madam*.

The concierge briefly consulted his register before looking up again. 'Yes, he booked a table for two. The valet will accompany you to the Red Ginger Lounge.'

'Thank you.'

'This way, please.'

Anita followed the young man, who looked uncomfortable in his immaculate cream suit with gold tassels sewn on each shoulder pad.

They crossed the sleek lobby surrounded by water features with gurgling fountains and headed towards the bar facing the sea. The area was bedecked with clusters of fresh bird of paradise in tall vases.

A friendly waiter led Anita to a table overlooking the infinity pool and ceremoniously held the chair out for her. As she was a few minutes early, she decided to order a cocktail made with rhum arrangé, a golden mixture infused with aromatic spices, including split vanilla pods and cinnamon sticks. It was a hotel speciality, the attentive young waiter assured her. He didn't even look old enough to drink.

Her cocktail arrived promptly in a tall glass. A copious amount of rum had been served over a mountain of crushed ice. Instead of a stirrer, it was accompanied by a long piece of raw sugar cane garnished with a fresh sprig of mint. It looked almost too pretty to drink.

Discreet lounge music floated in the air. In the far corner, a band was slowly setting. Glancing around the open-air lounge, Anita felt slightly out of place as she took in the tourists, dressed so confidently one would think they owned the world. She was glad she had settled on a sleeveless tunic dress made of raw silk, which she had managed to salvage from her old clothes. At the last minute, she had strung a chain of colourful beads around her neck and wrapped her bare shoulders with her favourite bottle-green pashmina, a gift from Ma after her last trip to India. The coral bracelet from Maya adorned her naked arm. Instead of her usual flats, she was wearing a new pair of strappy, heeled sandals she had bought in a moment of impetuosity. The shoes felt tight with the thin straps digging uncomfortably into her slim ankles. Her feet were starting to swell from the heat.

Quietly sipping her drink, she observed the tourists around her. Most of them were couples who looked as if they were either on honeymoon or celebrating a significant anniversary. They seemed so happy that it made Anita feel a little dejected as she realized just how alien that emotion had become. Or perhaps their happiness was only a facade. She knew nothing of their private lives. After all, who knew what went on once the glossy outer layer had been scraped away to reveal the core? Sometimes she would pick a ripe guava from Ma's garden, its exterior smooth and perfect to the touch, only to find that it was full of bebet, worms.

Anita thought about her own honeymoon. After their wedding, Paul had suggested using the cash they had received from their guests in lieu of wedding gifts as a deposit for a new car. Uninterested in gadgets, Anita had let him choose a model he had been admiring for a while. Instead of a lavish holiday, they had ended up backpacking their way around Thailand. They lodged in thatched one-room beach huts on stilts, off the beaten track, where they were often mistaken for students instead of newly-weds.

She recalled eating freshly made pad thai from the street vendors on Khao San Road in Bangkok, and drinking cheap wine from plastic cups under the stars as they philosophized about life. On Koh Pha-ngan, after a meal of grilled fish with fresh ginger and lemongrass, they had walked back to the beach hut, giggling from too much wine, and made love before falling asleep on top of the sheets, misted in sweat, letting the ceiling fan cool their naked bodies.

Her mind was awash with images of their former life. Back then, their budget honeymoon had felt like an adventurous way to begin their married life. She had been perfectly happy to lose herself completely in Paul. But had she mistaken lust for love? Had she imagined the happy years they'd spent together?

At their wedding reception, Paul had gazed at her with both lust and adoration while she glided around the marquee as gracefully as she could, draped in her silk wedding sari. She couldn't remember when he had stopped looking at her like that. On the frosty morning he had left, he had barely glanced at her. 'I've put down a deposit on a flat in Islington,' he'd said, 'but you're free to stay in the house until the divorce. I'll pick up the rest later.' And just like that, he had lugged his over-night bag out of the house and slammed the door behind him. Without looking back, he had climbed into the car and swerved off into the London traffic with a loud screech of tyres. She had no idea how long she had remained crouched against the radiator, sobbing with her head between her knees, until it became completely dark and she felt numb and cold.

Tired of looking at the seemingly happy couples around her, Anita took a sip of her drink and stared at the horizon. The sky, an abstract painting of mauve with a few wispy cirrus clouds, had a calming effect.

A few minutes later, at half past six exactly, Sven walked through the lounge in a pair of dark fitted jeans and a pale-blue shirt. She noticed the way he commanded respect without being imposing. He scanned the tables, looking for her, and smiled as he located her, hidden between two potted palm trees, quietly nursing her drink.

He greeted her with a casual peck on the cheek. 'Hallo.' There was a faint smell of alcohol tinged with mint on his breath. 'Have you been waiting long?'

'No, I got here a few minutes ago and already got myself a special rhum arrangé, as recommended by the barman.' She waved her glass. The alcohol was helping her relax.

The waiter stood a few discreet paces away, ready to take Sven's order.

'I'd like a gin and tonic please.'

When Sven's drink arrived, she liked how his hands gripped the crystal glass proffered by the hovering waiter: sturdy wrists with long, slender fingers and neatly cut nails.

He seemed more relaxed without Maya around constantly seeking his attention. They chatted as they ordered more drinks. Anita found it easy to talk to him, especially after the alcohol she'd consumed on a practically empty stomach.

Before Anita knew it, the words flooded out of her, as if someone had unlocked a door deep inside. It was the first time she'd talked openly about why she'd had to leave. Not wishing to dwell on the details, she tried to present the facts, trying hard to sound neither blasé nor overemotional. She twisted and knotted her hands in her lap as she spoke, and waited for a flicker of surprise to cross Sven's face, but he remained perfectly poised throughout.

As he listened, he leaned forward slightly and watched her intently, giving her his full attention. The way his kind blue eyes did not seem to judge or blame felt reassuring. 'I'm sorry if this is painful for you,' he finally said.

'It's the first time I've been able to talk about it.' Anita folded her hands in her lap, aware of a strange but welcome sense of release.

'Has it been helpful being here?' Sven asked, indicating the island with his hand.

Anita took her time before responding. 'I think so.' She nodded slowly. 'But sometimes I feel like I'm drifting. Floating in an unknown sea. It's hard to explain.'

'Sorry, I didn't mean to pry.'

'You're not. Distance somehow puts a new perspective on things.' She took another sip of rum and realized she was feeling dizzy. 'Will you please excuse me for a minute?'

Sven quickly got up and pulled the chair out for her. Not having worn high heels for a while, Anita walked unsteadily across the lobby to the ladies, conscious of his eyes fixed on her.

Once in the toilets, the flushed reflection in the gilt-framed mirror above the sink looked as if it had been imprinted with the dye of another being. To dismiss the thought, Anita splashed some cold water on her face and felt a little better. Then she washed her hands with soap, enjoying the rush of running water over her skin. She sat on a chaise by the dressing table and pressed a fluffy white towel to her temples, breathing in its fresh lemony scent. Rummaging through her bag, she found an old tube of mascara and applied a fresh coat to her already thick lashes, trying to steady her hands so as not to smudge it. Leaning close to the mirror, she dabbed on a thin layer of pearly lip gloss.

She had some trouble choosing from the bottles arranged on a bamboo tray with their labels neatly facing out. In the end, she sprayed herself with the complimentary eau de cologne and smeared her palms with coconut-scented cream.

The sides of her pashmina billowed softly in the mild breeze coming from the ocean when she made her way unsteadily back to their table. With a deep breath she raised her glass to her freshly glossed lips.

'Are you okay?'

'Oh, I'm fine. Just a bit dizzy.' Anita waved her hand dismissively.

'Are you unwell? Should we leave?' There was a look of concern on his face.

'It's the drinks and the heat. I hardly ate anything today, and the alcohol went straight to my head.'

'Then we'd better fix that.' Sven motioned to the waiter. Within seconds, the latter appeared in front of him with two thick leather-bound menus. 'Right,' he said, flicking through the pages. 'What do you fancy?' He looked up to meet her gaze. For a brief second, Anita wondered if his question was an innuendo.

'I don't think I can take anything too heavy right now. It'll have to be something light.'

'How about a seafood gratin and a side salad? It's deliciously light and fluffy. You'll feel better afterwards.'

Anita nodded. 'Sounds very tempting.'

'And I'll have the creamy lobster pasta,' Sven said to the waiter, who wrote down their orders.

'Would you like some wine with your meal, sir?'

'Yes please.'

Anita picked up a loose braid from her pashmina and started winding it around her finger as she observed Sven studying the wine list. The scar near his eye seemed more pronounced when his brow was creased in concentration. She pictured herself tracing it with the tip of her finger and gently blowing on it, the way Ma used to console her whenever she hurt herself as a child.

Sven looked up, interrupting her reverie. 'Do you like South African wine?'

'I do.'

'Then let's get the Chenin blanc from Stellenbosch. I think it'll go well with pasta and seafood.'

'Perfect,' Anita said, wondering how much more alcohol she could consume.

During their meal, bolstered by the wine, she interrogated Sven about his life in Germany. He told her he had had an uneventful childhood, growing up with his sister and parents in a village near Heidelberg where both his parents worked as educators. He had later moved to Hamburg, where he studied and worked for a few years. A big construction contract in the hotel industry had brought him to Mauritius, where he met Maya's mother, a Mauritian working for one of the leading resorts on the island. 'We were definitely not ready to start a family,' he admitted, looking down at his open palms. 'But one thing led to another, and soon enough she fell pregnant. I thought I'd do the decent thing and marry her, especially as she comes from a conservative Catholic family.'

He took another bite of his food before carrying on.

'But it was clear we were incompatible as a couple, and the cultural differences didn't help. Vanessa had never left the island before I'd met her. She had always lived in a world of her own.' He put down his knife and fork and studied the horizon.

Sven went on to tell Anita about the demanding projects he had been assigned, especially at the beginning, when he was still new and felt he had to prove himself. He had been busy putting together a competitive call for tenders, which his company ended up winning, but it took so much of his time that he hardly had any energy left for his family.

Anita could picture him in an office full of architectural drawings on easels and framed etchings on the walls. She imagined him with a small frown of concentration as, shoulders bent over a drafting table, he drew elaborate building plans.

'One day, I came home from a business trip to discover that my wife had moved out to her parents' place in Albion, taking Maya with her. It was apparently all too much for her to cope with.' He raised his napkin and dabbed his mouth before dropping it limply onto his lap.

'It can't have been easy,' Anita said. She swished the wine around in her glass and took another sip.

'Things were very tense between Vanessa and me, even on the good days. Living with her was like walking in a field of unexploded landmines. It wasn't a good atmosphere for a child to grow up in. She was eventually diagnosed with postnatal depression.' He stopped talking, seeming unsure of how to continue.

'Who has custody of Maya?' she asked between mouthfuls of gratin.

Sven was silent for a while as he finished chewing. 'We have not yet finalized the divorce. It's been taking a lot longer than expected.' He purposefully avoided looking at her.

Anita's fork paused on its way to her mouth. It remained poised in mid-air. There was an uneasy silence as Sven contemplated the bottom of his empty glass. The candle at the centre of the table flickered in the breeze, threatening to go out. As she watched him fiddle with his napkin, she wondered about the extent of his present relationship with the mother of his child.

Sven quickly changed the subject when the waiters came to clear their empty plates away. 'Would you like some coffee or dessert?'

'No thanks, I've had more than enough. I don't think I can manage anything more.'

He beckoned the waiter and settled the bill, leaving a generous tip for the latter, who thanked him profusely.

'Should we go for a walk?'

Anita gathered her bag and pashmina and followed Sven unsteadily down the stone steps leading to the beach, away from the hotel. Light music played by the hotel band floated in the background. A few glass lanterns, hanging from bamboo poles, lit their path.

They walked on the sand, listening to the gentle sounds of the waves caressing the shore. The sky was scattered with bright stars, and the moon cast its shimmering light across the water. Every now and then their arms brushed lightly.

After a while, Anita's sandals were biting into her skin. She bent down and almost lost her balance. 'Careful!' said Sven, grabbing her arm to steady her. His grip felt reassuringly strong. 'Perhaps you should sit down for a minute. Shall I get you some cold water?'

She shook her head and sat down on the sand facing the sea. It was refreshing to feel the gentle breeze on her flushed face.

'Take a few deep breaths.' Sven crouched down until his face was level with hers.

A moment later, Anita felt Sven's lips on hers and his arms around her neck. When she felt his weight against her, pushing her down, something deep inside snapped. 'Please stop this!'

Sven immediately pulled away from her, dropped his hands and took in what had happened. 'Anita, I thought...'

His face, towering above hers, sobered her up almost instantly. 'I must go.' She quickly stood, grabbing her sandals.

'Look, I didn't –' Sven started apologetically, unable to look her in the eye.

Without waiting for him to finish his sentence, she turned away and dashed back towards the hotel, throwing a 'Thank you for the meal!' over her shoulder as she ran. She was aware that barefoot, she would be much faster on the sand than Sven, who was wearing moccasins.

'Anita. Wait! Warte!'

She rushed past the late diners and went straight to the reception desk. 'A taxi please. Now!' she ordered, slightly out of breath.

'Certainly. We have a line of taxis waiting outside.' The concierge seemed acutely aware of her discomfort and feeling of urgency.

'Thank you.' She was relieved she didn't have to face Sven again. Within seconds, a vehicle glided in front of the lobby.

The attendant rushed to open the door for her. She jumped into the taxi without glancing backwards and ordered the driver to leave immediately.

'Anita! Wait. Warte!' She could still hear Sven's voice as the door snapped shut.

Once Anita had barked out Ma's address to the puzzled driver and caught her breath, she sank into the leather seat and covered her face with her clammy palms.

No matter how hard she tried to block it out, the professor's red face kept appearing in her mind, invading her thoughts, her entire being. Towering above her. Pinning her down.

The nausea resurfaced like the unwanted memories she thought she had buried deep inside, scenes replaying in her head. Shame pressed her shoulders down until they ached. How much longer would she be able to lie to herself and pretend it had never happened? When would the images finally stop haranguing her?

It was not until Anita was back in her bedroom that she realized what she had lost: her favourite pashmina, the one that had for years kept her warm and shielded her from the wind and rain. She knew it could be replaced a hundredfold, and yet she felt as if she had left a piece of herself behind. She could picture it lying limply on the deserted beach, lonely and abandoned, as if washed ashore after a shipwreck.

She peeled off her dress, which she balled up in her hands and threw into a corner of the room. Mascara ran in thick trails down her cheeks, staining her pillowcase and leaving dark shadows beneath her eyes.

19

The next morning, unable to sleep, Anita was up at dawn. She reached for the glass of water next to her bed and took a sip. Her mouth was painfully dry and her throat ached. The air reeked of rotten mangoes. She got up, took a quick shower, and decided to go on a pilgrimage to the south.

After taking a bus to Baie du Cap, she caught another one that rumbled and lurched along the coastal road to the village of Souillac, where she got off at the terminal near the Charles Telfair botanical garden.

She crossed the deserted street, walked past the wrought-iron gate and made a brief stop at the stone trough in the middle of the garden. She sat on an empty bench overlooking the ocean, next to a concrete slab advising visitors not to swim in the dangerous currents.

The scenery in the south was wilder than that on the rest of the island. Someone had once told her it was not uncommon for troubled souls to seek refuge in the wilderness.

Gloom descended upon her as she contemplated the rough sea below. An old Indo-Mauritian fisherman sat among the rocks, patiently holding his fishing rod. He had a kind face, lined with gentle, happy wrinkles – as if he had spent his whole life smiling and waiting for something good to happen.

From her seat, she had a clear view of Souillac's famous graveyard, which dated back to the times of French settlers.

After a while, Anita got up from the bench and followed the steps that led to the deserted patch of sand nestled between the basaltic rocks. As the waves pounded at her feet, she wondered how it would feel to immerse herself in the deep currents and to simply let go. To surrender to the sea. To float weightlessly, like a piece of driftwood, completely untethered. How easy it would be to let herself be swept away. Standing reverently in front of the ocean, she allowed the waves to spray her with cool water, like a pious disciple being blessed by a pandit. She wished she had an offering for the ocean, as would be expected of a dutiful devotee. Perhaps she could deliver herself to its depths in the form of a human sacrifice. As propitiation for the savage god of the sea. An offertory. A tribute to the divinity of water. *La mer capricieuse*. *La Preneuse*. The capricious sea, taker of human lives.

Strands of hair flapped around her face in the wind. Discarding her sandals, she dug her left foot into the coarse sand and felt pieces of shell and coral being sucked beneath it. The sand was scarred with rills. With her right foot, she formed semicircles on the shore and reminisced about the last time she had visited Souillac.

It must have been a Sunday when the family went out for the day to mark the end of her sister's A-level exams. Ma had cooked a big pot of fish biryani for the occasion, which they ate under the shade of a banyan tree, washed down with tepid Coca-Cola. Pa spiked his own drink with a generous amount of whisky, then dug into the pocket of his brownish trousers to fish out some money for the girls. He was in his usual attire, a well-pressed short-sleeved shirt and polyester trousers, clothes he had worn every day and still wore in Anita's memory. 'Go and buy some sorbet,' he said.

Delighted, Anita ran over to the marsan, proudly waving a note in the air, whereas Didi pocketed her share of the money, refusing to spend it on something so frivolous. Anita quickly ate the fistful of shaved ice garnished with cloyingly sweet red syrup as it melted into a treacle that dribbled everywhere.

Afterwards, Anita washed her sticky hands and mouth in the ocean, Ma and Pa hovering nearby. 'Careful, don't go in! The currents are very dangerous here,' Ma shouted as Anita approached the water and dipped her hands in and out before fleeing from the mighty waves as fast as she could.

When she was a child, her maternal grandmother, who lived in a nearby village near Saint-Aubin, had told her that the sea whispered its deepest secrets to those who could decipher its language and that its water was the cure to everything. But then again, Nani had always been a bit crazy, the pagli woman whose head was in the clouds. And even more so after the death of her daughter by suicide. From the snippets of hushed conversation overheard when she was growing up, Anita had pieced together the story of her aunt's illicit liaison with a wealthy married man who lived in a nearby house with his wife and young children. He had led her aunt to believe he would leave his family and elope to Italy with her. With the help of a beginner's book bought in Curepipe, her aunt had secretly taught herself some rudimentary Italian, dreaming of the day they could be together freely. She eventually found out he had no intention of leaving his family for her. He had spun lie after lie. She had been nothing but a distraction for him.

Rumours began to swell, as did her depression. Shortly after enduring a backstreet abortion, she took her own life. The ordeal sucked the life out of Anita's young aunt, both literally and metaphorically.

*

Digging her bare foot deeper into the sand, Anita spotted something glimmering among the broken corals as it caught a sunbeam. She picked it up, wiped off the sand with her thumb and held the object against the light. It was a smooth piece of aquamarine sea glass. Its etched surface had been marked by the sea, the sun, the sand and the time spent waltzing in the salty waters.

As a child, Anita had collected similar pieces of half-buried sea glass which, according to Nani, were the tears of mermaids. She had treated the colourful fragments like prized offerings from the sea. And when Anita got older and no longer believed in mermaids, she called them her sea jewels.

Buoyed by the unexpected discovery and the resurfacing of long-forgotten memories, she strode towards the end of the shore, looking for more treasures. Whenever she found one, she dug it up, scrubbed off the sand with her fingers and washed it in salt water. Each piece had a particular shade, colour and smoothness depending on how long it had spent drifting in the ocean. It was surprising how someone's discarded, broken plates and bottles could be regurgitated by the sea as precious gems. Whenever she came across one that had not yet gone cloudy, or still had sharp edges, she dug a hole in the sand and buried it safely inside. Some of these broken pieces needed more time, so when they re-emerged they would be rounded and softened.

After having combed the beach for a while, Anita contemplated her catch of a dozen or so treasures as their translucence caught the afternoon rays. Even the white ones were not really white but pearlescent, the colour of misty clouds on a rainy day.

A small piece in the shape of a petal, tangled in rubber-like seaweed, caught her attention. It reminded her of frozen lakes in winter, like the ones nestled in the forests of the northern English countryside that she had visited with Paul in a previous life.

Anita was about to leave when she discovered a triangular nugget half buried in the sand, which she had almost missed. When she held it up to the light, it took on a subtle auburn glow. Upon closer inspection, she realized it must have been part of a Phoenix beer bottle. The piece was slightly battered and misshapen but a treasure nevertheless.

She carefully wrapped her colourful little jewels in her towel, which she secured at the bottom of her bag before retracing her steps back towards the garden. There was a small make-shift stall on her way, where she bought a roti filled with butter bean curry. The middle-aged vendor seemed eager to engage in conversation. Anita responded to her pleasantries with a few absent-minded nods. The vendor tucked the edge of her sari around her pot belly before setting out to cook on a rudimentary stove. Using her bare fingers, she rotated the edges of the roti on the hot tawa until the dough puffed up to perfection.

Anita ate the roti quickly, while it was still hot, tasting the flavour of the curry mixed with freshwater shrimp chutney. She downed a glass of home-made tamarind juice with bergamot and wiped her hands on the greasy paper wrapper. On her way out of the park she flung the balled-up paper into the nearby bin, which a mangy dog was sniffing through, hungry for scraps; the animal let out a snarl before scampering off into the bushes.

As an afterthought, she went back to the stall and bought a gato mervey, which she bit into before leaving the garden and its stray animals behind. She then plodded towards the Robert Edward Hart Memorial Museum, where the poet had lived until his death.

Now, more than half a century after Hart's death, Anita was struck by the village's tranquillity as she wandered along its streets. Back in the day, Le Batelage had been a bustling harbour used by small cotiers for transporting sugar and other goods from the southern estates to the capital. Since the closing of the nearby sugar factories, the once lively port had become redundant.

She took a detour via the coastal cemetery that told the stories of lives lived, where famous counts and poets, notorious treasure-seeking corsairs and lesser mortals were buried side by side. Strolling past graves overgrown with wildflowers and epitaphs filled with sand, she stopped to read about 'Immigrant number 222317'. Who was this poor soul who had come from Bihar in the mid nineteenth century only for their life to end at Camp Bananes? Had they had a decent life, or were they better off here, listening to the peaceful sound of the waves?

Once she'd walked up the periwinkle-lined path to the museum and stepped inside Edward Hart's former cottage, Anita was overwhelmed by the atmosphere of a bygone era. Everything was frozen in time: the single bed with its faded, flowery bedspread, the veneered wood panels, even the musty smell in the air.

In the living room, she studied the paintings and the sepia pictures and wondered how it must have been to live on the island under French administration and later British rule.

There was a copy of the Holy Bible, a translation of the Quran and the Bhagavad Gita side by side on the ebony desk which faced the sea. One of Hart's poems particularly touched her as she read an excerpt:

Dans le bref crépuscule erre le Souvenir:
qu'il soit la vision près de s'évanouir

In the brief twilight memory wanders / like a vision, before fading away, she murmured. With the tips of her fingers, she stroked a heavy silver spoon and the rim of an antique blue teacup that had once touched the poet's lips. Deeply moved by the feeling of peace that reigned in Hart's former residence, Anita found herself in tears in front of the ocean that had greeted him every time he sat down to write odes to the sea. She stood for a while longer, enjoying the peace she felt, before leaving the cottage. As she approached the door, the friendly museum attendant handed her a pen and asked if she would sign the battered guestbook.

On the attendant's wooden secretaire was a display of vintage-style postcards that caught Anita's attention. Although she had no intention of writing to anyone, she rifled through them and stopped upon seeing a black-and-white one. It was an image of Paul and Virginie, from Bernardin de Saint Pierre's classic eighteenth-century novel, which she had read many years ago at school. She handed over some money and took the postcard.

Once outside the bungalow, Anita sat on the empty bench overlooking the sea, her hair flapping in the wind. She removed the newly purchased postcard from its envelope and studied the photo of the mythical lovers. It was a scene from the novel's famous *passage du torrent*: two teenage wanderers lost in the island's dense tropical forest. It was remarkable how, over time, this work of fiction – a story that had never taken place in real life – had come to be regarded as a significant event in Mauritian history. Although Virginie looks scared in the picture, Paul is smiling bravely for her sake. With his trousers and sleeves rolled up, he chivalrously carries his sweetheart on his back across the river, seemingly impervious to the slippery rocks as she clings to him for protection, her arms around his neck and her face almost buried in his wild, curly hair. Anita recalled the end of the book: Virginie's tragic death in the ship-wreck of the *St Géran* off the northern coast of Mauritius at Cap Malheureux, Cape of Misfortune. In the end, Paul cannot save Virginie from drowning.

Anita stared at the postcard for a long time, until the museum attendant came outside to inform her that they were about to close for the day. When he noticed her tear-stained face, he looked sympathetic. He placed his hand on her bony shoulders. '*Madame*,' he said. '*Ça ira*.' It will be all right. Translated literally, it meant 'It will go.' As he bid her farewell, Anita detected a hint of pity on his kind, wrinkled face. She wanted to stay there, in the fading light, for as long as she could, but eventually, hair wild with sea air and wind, she reluctantly got up and made her way back via Curepipe, a long and tiring ride.

Back at her mother's place, Anita went through the kitchen cupboards until she found an old apothecary jar with a cork lid. After cleaning it with hot soapy water and drying it with a tea towel until it shone, she filled it with her sea treasures and displayed it on her shelf, next to her favourite books.

While Ma was busy lighting a diya and cantillating verses for her evening prayers, Anita sneaked into her bedroom. It took her a few minutes to locate the wedding picture. Ma had hidden it in the bottom drawer of her lace-covered dressing table, among bottles of perfume, talcum powder and pots of Vicks VapoRub. Fiddling with the heavy frame, Anita used her fingernails to bend open the metal tabs before removing the picture stuck between the protective glass panel and cardboard passepartout.

Unable to look at the happy faces of the couple on their wedding day, she tore the picture into pieces and threw the scraps into the nearby bin. Before putting the frame back into the drawer, she replaced the earlier picture with the black-and-white postcard of Paul and Virginie. One set of mythical lovers replacing another.

2 O

Shadows were dancing on the sand of Tamarin Bay, where Anita sat cross-legged under a casuarina tree like a yogi. She was engrossed in her book when a flicker of shade fell across the pages. There was a man towering over her, his face illuminated by the sun. She squinted up at him, using her hands to block some of the light.

Sven was sporting bright-orange swimming trunks that showed off his tan. He was effortlessly carrying a surfboard under each arm. The glare of the sun magnified the silvery colour of the scar near his left eye, making it look surreal. 'Hallo Anita. May I join you?' He smiled sheepishly.

Feigning indifference, she returned her attention to the book, although she was unable to concentrate. Her body tensed up as he sat on the sand next to her.

'So this is where you've been hiding these last few days!' Sven exclaimed. 'Did you receive the parcel I sent you a few days ago?'

Anita reluctantly closed the book and looked him straight in the eye. The sunlight filtering through the trees cast a spider's web on his face, highlighting his scar. 'Yes, I did. Thank you for returning my pashmina. Would you mind? I'm trying to read.' She opened the book again.

'To be honest, I was hoping to return it in person,' he confessed.

She looked at Sven, not sure if she had heard him correctly. 'Excuse me? How fucking presumptuous of you!' From the corner of her eye, Anita noticed a crab shoot furtively out of a nearby hole. The creature scuttled sideways on the sand, clicking its pincers.

'Look, Anita. I –'

'You think buying me a fancy meal gives you the right to come on to me?'

'I misread the situation.'

'You knew I wasn't feeling well. Yet you chose that particular moment to make a pass at me? You took advantage of my weakness. What kind of a person does that?'

'I admit that my timing was appalling.'

'And you didn't even apologize.'

'I've been trying to! Like I said, I was hoping to see you, and then you didn't show up the last couple of days, so I had your shawl sent to you. I called several times, but your mother said you were indisposed.'

'Bloody well right I was.'

'Look, I'm really sorry for my behaviour. You will recall that I also had a few drinks that evening. I wasn't thinking straight.'

'And that's your excuse?'

'No, I'm just saying that I acted stupidly.'

'Yes, you did.'

'I'm not proud of my behaviour. It was completely out of character. I was hoping to make it up to you by taking you surfing.'

'What makes you think I'd want to go surfing with you? Anyway, I'm busy.'

'I see. In that case I'll leave you to it.' With a sigh, Sven picked up his board. 'If you don't want to talk to me, fine, I understand. But at least come by and visit Maya. She has

grown very fond of you, and I would hate to be in the way.
I know I messed up, but I had no intention of offending you.'

Unable to stay still with the thoughts hammering in her head,
Anita eventually picked up the board Sven had left behind.
Making sure he had completely disappeared from view, she fas-
tened the leashes around her ankles and paddled out into the
bay.

A few tries later, she jumped up and managed to catch the
crest of a wavelet. She slowly rose to her feet and stood tri-
umphantly, guided by the undulations of the sea.

Lifted by a swell, Anita felt the exhilaration of being on
top of the ocean, riding the waves, in tune with nature. But
the feeling of freedom was short-lived. In no time, the clouds
began to darken and she glimpsed a flash of lightning. And
before she knew it another surfer materialized out of nowhere,
gliding dangerously close to her. The other figure, rolling on an
approaching wave, looked vaguely familiar.

Anita tried to take a closer look at his shadowy face while
struggling to manoeuvre the board. She gasped and almost
lost her balance when she realized. 'Paul? Is that you? What
on earth are you doing here?' she shouted above the roaring
waters.

'Anita!' he called out to her, but the rest of his words were
lost in the wind.

A sharp thunderbolt. A gigantic wave, much bigger than the
others, rolled in, unbalancing her, and she was dragged under-
water and spun around in a sudden maelstrom. Desperately, she
clawed at the air, trying to breathe. Her eyes and mouth filled
with brine. The dark, treacherous ocean heaved her up and
down like driftwood.

Then Sven's bright-orange shorts flashed above the water. She tried calling out his name, but only a gurgle came out as the tumbling surf tried to swallow her.

A roar in her ears. Utter blackness. The ocean was closing in over her head, pulling her body down, its water murky and full of eel-like seaweed which tangled itself round her.

Surfing side by side, both Paul and Sven desperately tried to reach her. Sven managed to turn his board, but an arching wave broke over him and hauled him into the sea. Paul was next. In horror, she watched them disappear.

Frantically fighting the water, she was on the point of being swept away by a strong current when someone grabbed her hand and gripped it so tight that it hurt. She couldn't see the face, but she knew it was a man. It wasn't Paul or Sven, and yet his presence felt familiar and reassuring. She felt her soul leave her body and let herself be carried away.

The first thing Anita noticed was the blinding light, and that everything around her was blurred. A male figure was hovering above her. She realized she was in bed.

'Who are you? How did I get here?'

'Don't worry, you're safe.' The words sounded like they came from far away.

'Thank you for saving me,' she murmured.

'Don't thank me. You're not ready yet.'

She tried to make out his face, but all she could see was his outline.

'Are you a doctor?'

He didn't reply, but his presence felt comforting.

'I'm so tired. Can you help me get home?'

'I will. But there's something you need to do first.' Turning away from her, the man began to leave the room, and she realized he was wearing a short-sleeved shirt and polyester trousers.

A childhood memory surfaced.

'Pa, is that you?'

The lights dimmed and the room was left in darkness.

Anita woke up in a cold sweat. She felt bereft. Her right arm was stiff from having slept in an awkward position. She switched on the night light and, in three big gulps, finished the glass of water next to the bed. Still thirsty, she ventured into the semi-darkness of the house for some more water. Then she sat down on the kitchen floor. The linoleum was cool against her bare legs where her T-shirt had ridden up. With her head resting on her knees, she listened to the quiet hum of the house and the gentle purr of the refrigerator.

It was early in the morning when Ma knocked on her door before venturing in.

'Anita.'

'What is it?' Anita muttered, still groggy from sleep. The air felt heavy and charged.

'It was your sister on the phone,' Ma announced.

'Oh no, not again! Please. I've already told you, I don't want anything to do with her,' Anita mumbled from beneath the cover.

'It's important. You really have to speak to her.'

'No! I have nothing to say to her, or that husband of hers.'

'She's threatening to drive all the way from Balaclava if you don't call her back,' Ma pleaded.

'Fine then. Let her drive here. She can do whatever she wants, but I refuse to speak with her. I'm going back to sleep. Please close the door behind you.'

Ma, undeterred, hovered nervously around the bed. 'It's something to do with Nisha,' she announced quietly, as if speaking to herself.

Anita finally flung off the bedcover and sat up. Her insides twisted at the unexpected mention of her niece. 'What about that slut?' she asked, taking in her mother's drawn face and red eyes. The older woman sighed and lowered herself onto the bed.

With a sense of foreboding, Anita adjusted her position to make space for her mother, who sought out her hand from underneath the crumpled sheets. The weight of the two bodies made a sunken curve in the soft mattress.

Ma closed her eyes and opened them again, as if summoning up the energy and courage to continue. 'Look, Anita. This isn't easy.' She paused between sentences, carefully choosing her words.

'What's going on?' Anita looked at her mother's face, searching for clues. Ma appeared defeated.

'This might come as a shock, but I think you should know that she's expecting.' Ma spoke slowly and deliberately, like she would to a sick child.

'Expecting what?' Anita blinked a couple of times, unable to comprehend what Ma was trying to tell her. The air was thick with dread and her mother still refused to meet her eyes. Her words were left dangling in the air like a fishing line unable to hook the catch.

Then the meaning of the words finally hit her as the room seemed to swell. A deep, sickening feeling washed over her and then receded, like the water in the ocean before a storm.

The dense tropical air was oppressive. Tiny beads of perspiration appeared on her upper lip, and she started to tremble. Everything went blurry. Her view began to narrow as the walls closed in on her. She felt a pair of strong hands on her shoulders. The room went pitch black. Then silence.

A little later on, she heard light footsteps, followed by whispering. A damp cotton sheet, loose from its moorings, partly covered her feverish body. Somebody whose voice she could not recognize was in her room. He probed her a bit and gave her some pills to swallow. 'This should help with the shock.'

'Thank you so much for coming, doctor.' Ma sounded relieved.

'She's very weak. Make sure she stays hydrated, Mrs Ram, especially in this heat.'

The room went dark again as Anita began to drift in and out of consciousness. Random thoughts swam through her mind.

The days that followed felt purposeless, sterile. Countless hours passed by. Night and day, snippets of distant and not-so-distant memories came back in waves to haunt her.

Unable to sleep properly, Anita wallowed in the past, speaking to herself, asking questions that were left unanswered.

Every now and then came unfamiliar voices that she couldn't make out. At some point, she thought she heard her sister's voice in the background, followed by loud noises and echoes in her head. There were other times when the sounds were indistinct and muffled, as if heard through cloth.

Sometimes, it was Ma talking to the gardener outside her window, giving him tasks to do: clear away the rotten papayas, prune the breadfruit tree, protect the lychees from the greedy bats, fix the gate. Now and then, Ma would come into the room to light a mosquito coil to keep the night insects away.

While she lay there like a corpse, Anita was struck by how life was continuing as normal while she was caught somewhere between the living and not-living. 'How could he do that to me? She's my fucking niece! She was like the daughter I never had,' she mumbled, half delirious. Ma didn't answer. Instead, she smoothed away the strands of greasy hair from Anita's forehead and wiped her face with a cool damp cloth, while her daughter's hands curled on the sheet.

Whenever Ma came to rub coconut oil into her daughter's scalp, Anita wanted to hold her coarse hand and to breathe in its familiar smell, reminiscent of the sea and the earth and all the pious offerings and prayers she had carried out in front of the altar. But what had any of that achieved?

In a medicated haze, she noticed a bottle of pills on the table next to a bunch of fresh frangipanis, her favourite flowers, and a small card. It looked like a home-made bouquet, tied with a string of plain raffia. She wondered who it was from, knowing full well Ma would never do something so frivolous.

I see you like frangipanis?

They're my favourite flowers. There's something about their scent that reminds me of my childhood.

Aren't they supposed to represent new beginnings?

'What's that for?' she muttered, resurfacing briefly between naps.

'It's something to help you sleep better.'

She eagerly stretched out her hand for some more of the magic little pills that would give her a dreamless sleep – even if only for a few hours. It was slowly killing her just lying there in the dense tropical heat with thoughts going round and round in her head like the clock next to the bed constantly going tick, tick, tick.

Anita could not remember the last time she had slept without vivid nightmares of him and her: the other one. Whose name aptly meant *night*. Night, which meant darkness. The darkness of her niece's heart. Her own eighteen-year-old niece, whose studies she had generously sponsored and who she had welcomed into her home.

The day before Nisha's arrival in London, Anita had taken a detour to the Mauritian shop on Turnpike Lane to buy special ingredients and spices from her homeland. She had spent hours preparing an elaborate biryani in her niece's honour, and a separate meal for Paul. After work, Anita had accompanied

Nisha to Marble Arch to buy her a winter jacket from Marks & Spencer. They had stopped at Foyles in Charing Cross Road to pick up Nisha's university books as well as a copy of the *Student Survival Guide*, which Anita foolishly thought would help Nisha adapt to her new life in London.

Anita remembered those days as if they were sporadic scenes from a film. Paul's furtive glances as Nisha paraded around the house in her little negligee. Paul's innocent face as he volunteered to escort Nisha on his way to the City. Nisha flicking her lustrous hair. Paul in a sharp tailor-made suit and Italian brogues. Nisha, wearing cheap red lipstick and a strappy, skimpy top. Paul and Nisha as they made their way to King's College during Freshers' Week, stopping at a nearby pub for a quick drink on the way – or so he said.

She only had herself to blame for that nauseating ménage à trois, one that had happened right under her own roof. How could she have been so naive? She thought of the last time she had gone shopping with Nisha: she had even bought her niece lingerie with her credit card. Was Paul enjoying the lacy underwear that Anita had paid for?

Anita wondered if Paul was now taking Nisha to eat warm salt fish patties in the little Caribbean bakery behind Dalston market they used to go to. Was he helping her with her university assignments? Were they frolicking across the English countryside, or were they all loved-up in his flashy new Islington flat?

It was hard to swallow the fact that it had only taken a few months for her niece to fall pregnant and provide Paul with the life Anita had failed to offer him. The thought of her husband's legacy growing in her niece's womb left her sick with pain and grief.

Curled into a foetal position, Anita was unable to chase away the thoughts and images. Did Paul realize what he had done to her? Why Nisha, of all people? Most astonishing, in retrospect, was the way he had pursued her niece. All the time Anita had thought her husband was being kind and supposedly looking after her protégée – as she had asked him to – was he pondering his own treachery? Had he understood what he was doing, or had he operated on a subconscious level? Endless scenarios played out in her mind as she searched their seemingly innocent faces for clues to their subterfuge.

Had Paul been attracted to Nisha because she was as malleable as Anita had once been? Hadn't her style, mannerisms, tastes changed after meeting him? She had become a different person after leaving her other self behind, like she had simply shed a skin.

Keeping track of the days was difficult, but at some point Anita eventually managed to negotiate her way out of bed, only to float aimlessly from room to room, scarcely knowing what she was searching for or what time of the day or night it was.

Entering Port Louis overloaded Anita's senses – the welcome chaos that greeted her as soon as she descended from the express bus to the capital. The sudden rise in temperature, a familiar burst of colours and sounds, shoals of people, street hawkers shouting their wares right and left. Anita floated about the cobbled streets, narrow arteries that led to the heart of the city, where decrepit colonial houses with peeling walls stood out in defiance next to soulless new buildings. There were several lotel dite where coteries of older men could be seen poring over tabloids, smoking and drinking tea. She crossed the road to avoid a soular who was drunkenly urinating on a stone wall bedecked with peeling posters advertising adult movies being showcased in some shady cinema hall nearby.

Anita entered the small tabazi, aware she had some time to kill until government officials exited the headquarters for their lunchtime break. The shop was adjacent to an abandoned building with streaks of red paint running down its walls, as if the building was bleeding from inside. The few ferns hanging from the stone wall were scorched brown from the heat. The building's courtyard garden, once flourishing, was now dead.

After scanning the limited menu, hastily written on a blackboard behind the counter, she ordered dite disik and a sandwich. She sat in an empty seat next to the wall that gave her a clear view of the modern building across the street. It was not yet midday, but the young waitress who served her already looked haggard, resigned to the inevitable rush of customers that would pour into the restaurant-cum-shop as soon as the clock struck noon.

She held her spoon up to the light and inspected it, before taking out a tissue and wiping it of fingerprints and relics of earlier meals. The hovering waitress did not seem in the least insulted by her gesture. Her face had an expression that said: *As if I care.*

Anita felt her anxiety increase with each passing minute. There was a hollow feeling in the pit of her stomach that no amount of food or sweet tea could fill.

For want of something better to do, she picked up a battered tabloid that was clearly a few days old. She leafed through the grease-stained pages. A famous minister charged with corruption. A schoolteacher accused of molesting his young pupils. A Good Samaritan who had tried in vain to save the lives of a driver, his young daughter and their nanny following a traffic collision near Albion.

At some point she thought she recognized the haunting face of a woman pictured under the headline MAURITIAN WOMAN FOUND DEAD IN BATH IN LONDON, IN A POOL OF OWN BLOOD. She stared at the familiar face before tossing the paper to one side with a sinking feeling.

For the hundredth time, she turned around to look at the plastic clock on the wall and knocked over her untouched tea, which had now gone cold. 'I'm so sorry,' she said to no one in particular.

The waitress reluctantly picked up her dirty tea towel, came over and wiped the plastic table.

'Thanks,' Anita muttered.

'Are you waiting for someone?'

'Not really,' Anita lied. She didn't look up at the woman.

Choosing to ignore the waitress's hint, she remained in her seat for another good half-hour without taking her eyes off the building across the street. It wasn't until a familiar figure emerged from the main door that Anita left the shop.

She knew it was now or never, and deftly followed the woman, who was heading towards Rue Desforges. She called out, but there was no reaction. 'Wait!' she shouted, this time louder. The woman stopped in her tracks, body tensed.

She came face to face with her older sister, who looked as if she had seen a ghost.

'Anita!'

Anita looked her sibling in the face. 'Hello, Didi.'

'What the hell are you doing here?'

'You said you wanted to talk.'

'What? First you ignore my phone calls, and now you decide to ambush me here? In the middle of Port Louis, outside my workplace?'

The two women stared at each other, neither of them blinking or backing away.

'I was left with no choice,' Anita said.

'You have some nerve!' Didi hissed. There was something hysterical in her tone. Her face contorted in anger.

'We can't talk here. Let's go somewhere quieter.'

Reluctantly, Didi followed Anita's lead as they manoeuvred their way through Chinatown, finding shelter in a dark room at the back of a dodgy-looking arcade not far from Les Jardins de la Compagnie.

'You were supposed to look after my daughter! The one thing I asked you to do! She was in your care.'

'You think I didn't care for my only niece?' Anita retorted.

'Then tell me why she ended up getting pregnant. With your husband's child! Under your roof!' Didi spat.

'I don't know. I gave her everything. I welcomed her into my house, but not into my marriage,' Anita whispered to the table.

'She's a child herself!'

'You think I wanted this to happen? For my husband to leave me for my fucking niece, of all people?'

'What was Paul thinking?'

'I ask myself the same question every minute of the day.'

'You always had it all. The way Ma and Pa doted upon you. You were their favourite child.'

'That's not true.'

'You had everything! The scholarship, your career, your fancy house in London! Nisha was all I ever had.' Didi's eyes brimmed with tears.

'And having a child was all I ever wanted. I would have given it all away in a split second to know what it was like to be a mother.'

'Now I have nothing,' Didi sobbed into her handkerchief. 'I've lost Nisha to your husband.'

'And I've lost Paul to your daughter.'

Looking at the pain in her sister's face, Anita reached across the table and took Didi's hand. Only then did it occur to her that Didi was as broken as she was. For the first time in her life, Anita felt affection towards her sibling.

Afterwards, it was with a strange feeling of capitulation that Anita said her final goodbye to Didi. She watched her sister walk down the narrow streets of Port Louis until she disappeared completely, lost in the ever-flowing arteries of the capital.

Anita's steps felt lighter as she trod on the cobbled pavement, the ancient stones worn soft by centuries of pedestrians who on one day or another had taken that very same journey back home.

On the bus back to Palma, Anita thought of an image she had come across some years ago at the National Gallery in London. It was an oil painting depicting a peaceful scene: two girls on a boat. At the time, she had wondered whether it was a *trompe l'œil*, as she couldn't tell how deep the seemingly calm waters were.

Two girls on a boat, together and yet alone in their misery. As the motion of the bus lulled her to sleep, Anita wondered if life was simply another *trompe l'œil*.

23

The rain battered the windowpane in a cacophonous symphony. The sky was troubled and fragmentary, with claws of cirrus and stabs of lighting. Torrential water rushed through the streets, flooding the gutters, pounding everything in its way, unearthing chunks of cement from the pavements. Its obstinacy was relentless.

From bed, Anita watched the water coming down the walls slowly, seeping through the layers, penetrating invisible cracks. Drip. Drip. Drip. The sound was unnerving. She wondered when the wall would break and the water would take everything in its way.

As if in a trance, she walked out of the house in the dead of night to cleanse herself under the pelting rain, hoping for some sort of respite. She listened to the angry voices of the night. The stormy howls of the wind. The cracks of branches being ripped off trees, swept away at tremendous speed.

She stood motionless under the deluge for some time, letting the water mat her hair and cool her skull. Anita wished she could melt under the downpour like a lump of brown sugar, wash away until there was nothing left. Disappointed, she reluctantly went back indoors. She stripped off all her clothes and left them on the floor in a wet puddle before climbing back naked into bed. Wearing clothes was too constricting.

24

Anita rubbed her eyes. It must be morning, as she could hear Ma putting the kettle on and bustling about. She lay in bed for a few minutes, staring at her childhood ceiling and its familiar cracks, which were slowly starting to resurface despite the recent makeover.

Her messy hair was sticking unpleasantly to her back. After swallowing a couple of pills from the small plastic tub on the bedside table, she ventured into the kitchen to find Ma eating an atemoya and drinking tea from a steel tumbler. The sickly scent of overripe fruit and sandalwood filled the kitchen. Her mother had just finished her morning prayers; an incense stick was burning at the altar.

Ma's eyes lit up as Anita walked into the room hazy with smoke. 'How are you feeling?' she asked, quickly getting up from the table.

Anita shrugged in response.

'Would you like some tea? Or some fresh carambolas from the garden?'

'No thanks,' Anita mumbled, feeling slightly nauseous at the thought of food. What she yearned for was a long shower to wash her greasy hair and the reek of stale sweat off her ghoulish-looking skin.

Once in the bathroom, she could hardly recognize the drab, skinny woman who stared back at her in the mirror. She turned on the tap and stepped under the cold, baptismal blast, hoping the lump inside her would wash away and disappear down the drain like the grease from her skin. That the lethargy that plagued her would unwrap its tentacles from her frail body.

After her shower, Anita went to the kitchen and opened one of the cupboards. Once she found what she was looking for, she slipped the heavy object into her bag without Ma noticing. 'I think I'll go out for a bit,' she announced to no one in particular.

Ma hadn't heard her; she was too busy preparing a pain maison sandwich filled with leftover rougay.

'Don't bother. I'm not hungry,' Anita protested.

'Take it with you, you've hardly eaten a thing these last few days. It'll do you good. And don't be too long. You're still weak. The December heat is horrendous.'

Reluctantly, hair still wet, Anita squeezed the packed steel gardmanze into the bag and left the kitchen.

'Anita, wait! You forgot your book!' Ma shouted behind her.

She turned around to find Ma brandishing a paperback novel that had been gathering dust on her bedside table.

'No, I won't need it. Today I just want to read the waves.' Besides, there was no more room in her bag.

Ma let out a long sigh and shook her head.

When Anita finally stepped outside, she recognized the pungent smell of an overripe jackfruit in the garden. The shape of the heavy fruit, hanging off the branch, reminded her of a pregnant woman's belly. It looked somehow grotesque.

Her jeans and T-shirt hung loosely on her as she dragged her sandal-clad feet to the bus stop, her shoulders hunched. With every step she took she could feel the void beneath her feet.

Before she crossed the road, a truck carrying a load of sugar cane flew by, dropping a few stalks that were then crushed by a passing car. Anita trudged on through the sticky mess, oblivious.

Hoisting her heavy bag further up her shoulder, she climbed onto the bus towards Baie du Cap and settled at the back of the rattling vehicle. Plumes of distant smoke hovered above the sugar factory like snakes slithering through the sky.

As the wind dispersed the fumes towards the coast, Anita felt like she was watching her tarred soul drifting aimlessly in the wind. Dark trails of smoke evaporated into the atmosphere before being reduced to nothingness.

At Cascavelle, a young mother and her toddler boarded the bus. The little boy was wearing a Superman T-shirt and bright white trainers. Anita felt a pang when she noticed how the mother held her child's hand firmly so he would not lose his balance as they climbed into the vehicle. '*Trap mo lame for tansion to tonbe.*' Hold on to my hand so you won't fall. The woman only let go of the boy's palm once she had lifted his tired little body onto the seat and swaddled him tightly against her chest. After a while, rocked by the motion of the bus, the child fell asleep. He looked serene. Anita could not help but envy the mother.

Every now and again she caught a glimpse of the woman's face. She watched her push strands of hair away from the boy's eyes and caress his chubby cheeks. At La Gaulette, her arm no doubt stiff from the child's embrace, the woman gently disengaged herself by wriggling her body inch by inch. She deftly retrieved her arm, making sure her movements would in no way disturb her little boy's sleep. Anita felt deeply affected by that small act of motherly tenderness. Unable to stand the sight any longer, she got up and changed seats.

Anita used to dream of visiting Mauritius with her baby proudly displayed in her arms. All her friends had children:

school friends, university friends, colleagues, neighbours, cousins, family friends. Wherever she looked, there were pregnant women and happy mothers with a brood of children to remind her of her anomaly.

She had lost touch with these people, from whom the tide of life had long since separated, especially as her childlessness became a recurrent topic of conversation. She was asked again and again when it would be her turn, what she was waiting for – and should she really be having a glass of wine with her meal? It became too much for her to bear. Even Ma had pestered her for a time, craving a swarm of grandchildren to spoil and cherish in her older days.

Failure cloaked her like a mantle. She was aware of how much Paul wanted a family. And he would have been a good father to their children. So many times, he had told her not to worry, that it wasn't a problem, there were so many couples without children. Had she underestimated his need to pass on his family name?

After their wedding, they used to nurse quiet plans for their babies. She was certain Paul had daydreamed about kicking a ball in the garden with his son, just as she had fantasized about taking her daughter to ballet class. Soon, she'd thought, he would be able to proudly carry their child to the nearby park. Instead, he had fathered a child with her niece.

Anita was jolted back to the present when the bus halted at the terminal in Souillac, where she finally got off. She walked through the park, down the steps, past the secluded beach and the concrete slab with its warning. She found a quiet spot among the rocks and sat down, oblivious to the scorching sun above. There were no fishermen about due to the midday heat.

She contemplated the wide expanse of sky and sea ahead, wondering what could possibly lie beyond the horizon.

Feeling thirsty, she opened her bag and fished out the glass bottle she had sneaked into it before leaving the house. She swallowed a mouthful of the golden liquid and grimaced as it burned her throat.

For a split second, her father appeared in front of her, smiling as she took another swig of his favourite drink. His presence was a brief blur, like the occasional fish darting in and out of the seawater, making her wonder whether the apparition had been real. Pushing away strands of hair from her face, she decided to take a few more swigs, simply to show her father that she too could appreciate good whisky. He used to enjoy a few glasses every evening.

Even though the liquid burned her throat, she kept on drinking. She welcomed the alcohol into her system. Her head began to spin. The heat of the sun was becoming unbearable as she drank some more. The more she slugged, the more accessible the horizon seemed to be. From somewhere far away, the gentle song of the ocean called her, floated to her in waves, until she was no longer scared of its infinity.

The bottle slipped out of her hands and landed with a loud crash on the rocks, sending around a spray of golden liquid and broken glass. She smelled something metallic. Was she bleeding? She looked down at her hands. They were red; a warm, thick burgundy slowly oozed out of her wrists. She would rinse it off. Just a quick dip in the lagoon. The rocks were slippery, partly covered in green, velvety moss. The water felt cool and welcoming. If she could only lift her hand a little bit more, she would be able to touch the horizon. Just a bit more. Almost there. Infinity. It would be like walking on water. Water that slowly surrounded her, until she started to float free.

She saw her father again. He was smiling down at her. He looked young, unscathed by time.

'Here, beti, come with me.'

Anita accepted the hand he held out. His grip was cold and firm. The salt water closed in on her, absorbing her in its entirety, until she finally became one with the ocean.

EPILOGUE

It is a clear morning in December. The blue sky seamlessly blends in with the ocean. A remnant of rainbow lingers behind the mountain range. From the crowded observation deck of Sir Seewoosagur Ramgoolam International Airport, an older woman awaits the arrival of the aircraft. She seems oblivious to the rivulets running down her face.

The British Airways plane that left Heathrow twelve hours earlier slowly makes its descent before landing on the tarmac. The sight of the approaching aircraft distresses the woman, who looks as if she is about to faint. Another woman takes her hand and leads her gently away from the onlookers eagerly awaiting their loved ones. The passenger they are waiting for is the only one who will be wheeled out: a cold, metal casket, buried in the dark belly of the plane.

Once the formalities are over, and various documents signed, the older woman solemnly follows the doctor. She shivers and pulls her sari over her mouth before entering the morgue. The place reeks of chemicals and death.

'Are you ready, Chachi?' asks the doctor. The woman nods in response.

Respectfully, he opens the metal casket. The woman's face blanches as she sees her younger daughter under the cruel glare of the fluorescent light. She stands frozen in the face of death and then starts to sob quietly. 'What did you do to yourself?' she asks in a broken voice.

'We received the autopsy report. She was admitted to Homerton Hospital in Hackney, but it was too late to save her.'

'Wake up, please! Come back!' the woman begs.

'The cause of death was pulmonary oedema caused by water in the lungs.'

'Why, Anita? Why?' She leans over and gently traces the edges of her daughter's purple lips.

'There were high levels of alcohol in her blood. Both her wrists had been cut open.'

'My baby. My beti. Mouni!' she whispers to the corpse.

'She was found in the bath with an empty bottle of whisky and some sleeping pills on the floor.'

'You should have come home. I would have looked after you. Like when you were a baby.' She wants to lean over and kiss her daughter one last time, but the doctor stops her.

'I think that's enough, Chachi.'

She leaves the morgue in a trance, a mere shadow.

The morning air in Palma feels heavy. Bulbuls chirp in the trees at the back of the garden. There is a respectful silence as a group of male relatives hoist the palanquin made of wood and bamboo. A frangipani blossom falls off the skeleton of planks carrying the woman's body. Her feet are facing south according to religious customs.

Shifting the deadly weight on their shoulders, the corpse bearers slowly make their way through the cane fields towards the ocean below. They stop at the small Hindu temple, where a freshly stacked pyre is being prepared for the antyesti ritual.

The retinue of male mourners keep on chanting the mantra to redeem the dead from bad deeds.

Ram naam satya hai. Ram naam satya hai. Ram naam satya hai.

Ram. Ram. Ram naam satya hai. Ram naam satya hai.

Ram naam satya hai. Ram. Ram naam satya hai.

Anita Ram. Anita Ram. Anita Ram.

Anita. Ram.

Anita.

As the sun sinks below the horizon, Ma closes her eyes in prayer and slowly scatters the ashes into the sea. For a long time, she stands with her feet in the water, watching the waves gently carry the rest of her daughter into the bay of Tamarin.

THE END

Comme un goémon
J'ai dansé sur les flots
Et l'eau pénétra ma peau, mon âme
Nue, je me suis baigné dans la nature
Dévorant les azurs

I danced like seaweed on the waves
And water did seep into my skin, my soul
Laid bare, I swam in a nature
That devoured the horizon

PRIYA HEIN
(translated by Jeffrey Zuckerman)

Acknowledgements

I would like to thank my amazing agent, Anna Soler-Pont, and her wonderful team at Pontas Literary and Film Agency, especially Carla Briner and Clara Rosell, for being such enthusiastic champions of my work. A big thank you to my brilliant editor, Susie Nicklin, who understood me immediately and for her remarkable commitment to this book and herstory. My heartfelt thanks to everyone at the Indigo Press, especially Phoebe Barker for making my book shine and Sarah Terry for her thoroughness.

I am forever indebted to Ananda Devi, J.M.G. Le Clézio and Issa Asgarally for their continued support. To the very early readers of this novel: I am sorry you had to read (embarrassingly) early drafts or parts thereof: Ameerah Arjanee and Rita Banerjee at the Munich Readery Workshop, Mark Casali, Lindsey Collen, Lisa Ducasse, Corinne Fleury, Rebonto Guha, Sophie Jai, Yovan Mahadeb, Shenaz Patel, Barlen Pyamootoo, Bénédicte Robert Espitalier Noel, Tatiana de Rosnay and Haddiyyah Tegally. I appreciate all your feedback. I would also like to thank Christina Meetoo for reviewing the Creole texts.

Part of this book was submitted to and written during the 2019 University of Iowa's International Writing Program Women's Creative Mentorship Project and finalized during its 2024 IWP Fall Residency. I was lucky to be able to participate in both programmes thanks to the Bureau of Educational and

Cultural Affairs at the US Department of State, and would like to thank the US Embassy Mauritius for nominating me. My gratitude to Christopher Merrill, Cate Dicharry, Shelly Criswell, Mac Gill, Julieta Rangel Gómez, Ikram Basra, Mike Meginnis and Monique Galpin from the IWP: I look forward to returning your hospitality someday. To Karoline Kamel and Phodiso Modirwa: thank you for being there.

Much gratitude to my dear friends Andreas Bjørløw, Claudio Cumani, Florence Guillemain, Sara Hoffmann-Cumani and Dweena Saddul, who are always there for me. And also to Alexandra Bellon, Marianne Cantwell, Reza Dulymamode, Ari Gautier and Gaitee Hussain for their support.

Finally, thank you as ever and always, to Stefan, Ananya and Kian. You are my everything.

Transforming a manuscript into the book
you hold in your hands is a group project.

Priya would like to thank everyone
who helped to publish *Tamarin*.

THE INDIGO PRESS TEAM

Susie Nicklin
Phoebe Barker
Phoebe Evans

JACKET DESIGN

Luke Bird

PUBLICITY

Sophie Portas

EDITORIAL PRODUCTION

Tetragon
Sarah Terry
Alexander Middleton